WEREDUCK

Dave Atkinson

NIMBUS
PUBLISHING

Nimbus Publishing Limited
3731 Mackintosh St, Halifax, NS B3K 5A5
(902) 455-4286 nimbus.ca

Printed and bound in Canada

NB1141

Author photo: Neal Gillis
Interior and cover design, and illustrations: Jenn Embree

Library and Archives Canada Cataloguing in Publication

    Atkinson, Dave, 1978-, author
        Wereduck / Dave Atkinson.
    Issued in print and electronic formats.
    ISBN 978-1-77108-219-8 (pbk.).—ISBN 978-1-77108-220-4 (html).—ISBN 978-1-77108-221-1 (mobi)
        I. Title.

PS8601.T5528W47 2014   jC813'.6   C2014-903201-3
                                          C2014-903202-1

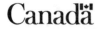  

Nimbus Publishing acknowledges the financial support for its publishing activities from the Government of Canada through the Canada Book Fund (CBF) and the Canada Council for the Arts, and from the Province of Nova Scotia through Film & Creative Industries Nova Scotia. We are pleased to work in partnership with Film & Creative Industries Nova Scotia to develop and promote our creative industries for the benefit of all Nova Scotians.

Erin once said she thought it might be kind of

fun to be a duck. This book is for her.

CHAPTER ONE

KATE EXAMINED THE REFLECTION OF THE FULL moon on the surface of the lake. She picked out the mountains and craters that give the moon its face—features that make it seem as if our closest neighbour in space is gazing back at us.

Kate tossed a rock into the water, spoiling the image. Tiny ripples radiated from the spot, eventually lapping against the shore. There, in the shadows of the trees at the lake's edge, she spotted a duck that had woken at the sound of the splash.

He lifted his head from under his wing and looked around. He stood up on skinny legs and puffed out his chest. Before stepping into the water, he wiggled his feathered butt.

Kate smiled. She loved that wiggle.

Kate unfolded her legs and stretched them before her on the ground. Her feet and toes tingled. Sometime in the last hour, they had fallen asleep.

The lonely howl of a wolf drifted above the top of the spruce forest. It was joined by another, and another.

A dozen or more ducks that were beside the lake awoke in a flutter of quacks. They waddled into the cool water and relative safety of the lake. Kate noted they didn't bother with the formality of butt wiggles.

The howling jarred Kate from her thoughts. She was awake much later than she'd planned to be. She pulled herself to her feet, stamping them a few times to beat out the pins and needles. She dug her hands into the pockets of her windbreaker and began the short walk around the lake.

The light of the moon dimly illuminated the cabin where her grandmother and brother slept. Her parents were busy tonight; she wouldn't see them until morning. Kate passed the campfire pit and saw that the embers had faded to black.

Kate pushed open the door to the cabin, being careful not to let it squeak on its rusty hinges. Her eyes took a moment to adjust to the darkness. Without the light of the moon, the cabin was dark as pitch, but there was no mistaking the pair of yellow eyes staring back at her. Kate stood frozen in the doorway.

The eyes belonged to a black wolf. Beside it on the ground, lay the motionless body of Kate's younger brother.

She took a bold step forward. "Grandma!" hissed Kate. "I thought I told you to save room for me."

Kate crawled between her sleeping brother and her furry grandmother. She nudged the boy out of her way like a wolf cub pushing out a competing sibling. Her grandmother let out the long sigh of a contented canine. Kate nuzzled into her thick dark fur.

"Goodnight," whispered Kate.

In a moment, she was asleep.

CHAPTER TWO

KATE'S GRANDMOTHER, MARGE, HAD THE CAMP-
fire going by the time Kate dragged herself out of bed
the next morning. She let the door swing back on its
spring and slam as loud as it could, knowing the noise
would surely wake her brother.

"You slept in your jacket again last night," Marge
said, not looking up from her breakfast preparations.
"It's going to be ruined with wrinkles." She opened a
cooler beside her and took out two of packages of bacon.
Slices of potato sizzled in a big iron pan suspended atop
a bed of glowing coals.

"It's nylon," replied Kate, smoothing the front of
her jacket with her hands, "nature's most forgiving
fabric. Is the tea ready?"

Marge laid aside the bacon and poured Kate a cup
of tea. She placed it in her hands and planted a kiss on
her forehead. "Happy birthday."

"Don't remind me," said Kate.

"You sound like you're turning thirty, not thirteen," laughed Marge. "It's not every day a girl becomes a wolf."

Kate took a sip from her steaming cup. She looked straight ahead.

"Unless," continued Marge, "that's a problem?"

"Are you sure there's no opt-out clause on this whole werewolf thing?" asked Kate. "I can think of better things to do with my time than running around the forest every month howling my head off."

Her grandmother smiled. "Such as?"

Kate looked away.

"You know as well as I do how it works, Katie dear," said Marge. "Our family has been wolves as far back as anyone can remember. I think you may come to like it."

Kate grabbed the flipper and poked at the potatoes. She pushed them aside in the pan to make room for the bacon.

"Why wolves?" asked Kate. "There's a reason why the angry mobs in the movies are always trying to kill werewolves—people hate us."

Marge smiled. "You have a better suggestion?"

Kate blushed. "Well," she began, "I always thought, maybe, it might be kind of fun to be a duck."

"A duck?"

"Yeah, why not?" said Kate. "Wouldn't it be cool? I mean, ducks, right? Fly, swim, waddle—they do everything! And they have this quiet dignity."

"Ducks," said Marge flatly, "have quiet dignity?" She raised her eyebrows.

"Tons!" exclaimed Kate. "And they do that butt-wiggle thing." Just as she jumped up to give her rear a little shake, the door to the cabin swung open. Her eleven-year-old brother stood watching with devilish delight.

"Katie Wereduck," Bobby announced. "You can wiggle that butt all you like. When that moon comes up tonight, you're going to be a wolf."

Kate grimaced. She folded her arms and plunked back down on her stump.

"You have no idea how lucky you are!" said Bobby. "Some of us have to wait a whole fourteen months, two weeks, and three days to turn into a wolf!"

"Some of us think there's more to life than chasing rabbits."

"Like wiggling your butt?" said her brother.

"That's enough butt-wiggling talk from the both of you," said Marge, slapping an empty plastic jug into Bobby's hands. "Go contemplate your inner wolf down by the spring while you fetch us some water."

He grabbed the jug. "Gladly, Grandma. *Ah-wooooo!*"

"Fleabag," muttered Kate as her brother tromped toward the woods.

"*Ah-wooooo,* Bobby!" came a new voice.

Kate and Bobby's dad, Brian, bounded up from the forest. His hair was a wild tangle of twigs and dirt. Their mum, Lisa, similarly disheveled, followed a few steps behind, tucking in a stray corner of her shirt.

"*Ah-wooooo,* Dad!" yelled Bobby, nearly hopping into his father's arms. "How was it? Did you chase rabbits? Did you find any deer? How far'd you go?"

"Hold on there, cub," said Brian, giving his son a hug. "We can talk when you get back with your grandma's water. Hurry up, we're going to have a couple of new werewolves join us for breakfast."

"Are you serious? Other wolves?" asked Bobby. His eyes bulged.

"Serious," said his mother, Lisa. "You can meet them in a few minutes."

Bobby dashed into the woods.

"What a night," said Lisa, collapsing on one of the stumps surrounding the fire. "I was going to throw myself on my bunk and sleep all day—until I thought of your potatoes, Mum. Is there tea?"

"There's always tea," said Marge. She poured a cup for Lisa and another for Brian.

"Thanks, Marge," he said.

"What's this about other wolves?" asked Kate. "I thought we were the only werewolves around here."

"So did I," said Brian. "Surprise, surprise." He blew on his tea and took a sip.

"I thought I heard extra howls last night," said Marge. "From the south. The other side of the river."

"Yeah, that's where we found them," nodded Lisa. "Or found each other, I guess. We chased each others' howls for a while before finally meeting."

"And what are they like? Are they nice?" asked Kate.

"Well, they're nice *wolves*," said Brian. "So, they like chasing rabbits and running around and howling. We only met them as people when the sun came up. They were just stopping at their own camp before joining us. They should be right behind us."

"How many are there?" asked Kate.

"Two," said Brian. "A father and son."

There was a rustle from the woods as Bobby returned. Climbing the hill with him were two extra figures.

"Speak of the werewolf..." said Brian.

Kate sat pinned to her stump as they approached. Bobby chatted a mile a minute, skipping sideways to keep up with the newcomers.

"So, oh my gosh, I totally can't believe you're werewolves, too. Dad said we were the only ones around here."

"We're pretty new to the area," said the father: a dark-haired man with grey eyes.

Kate assessed the son. He was maybe fifteen. He had his dad's eyes, but had rusty brown hair that looked about a month overdue for a cut.

Not exactly cute, thought Kate. *But not not-cute, either.*

"I'm sorry," announced the father politely as he approached the fire. "We haven't met everyone yet. I'm Marcus," he shook Marge's and Kate's hands. "This is my son, John."

"Hey," said the boy. He reached out to shake hands with Kate. His grey eyes looked briefly into her brown.

"Hi," she said. She held his glance for just a moment then looked at the ground. *Okay, maybe a little cute,* she thought.

CHAPTER THREE

Two days earlier, a newsroom in New York City

DIRK BRAGG RANSACKED HIS DESK, GRABBING seemingly random objects and stuffing them into a duffel bag: Six pads of paper. A pair of socks. A telescopic camera lens. Half a pastrami sandwich.

He looked a mess. He wore a rumpled, tan dress shirt tucked sloppily into a pair of khaki pants—themselves fifteen years past their fashion expiry date. His face was unshaven. His messy hair was vaguely parted to the left.

"Where are you off to in such a hurry?" came a woman's voice from across the newsroom. Dirk looked up and saw his editor, Sandra, pouring herself a cup of coffee.

"Canada," grunted Dirk, throwing a box of pencils into his bag. "New Brunswick."

"Canada?" she asked. "What would you want to go there for?"

Dirk stuffed what looked like a six-week-old banana into his bag. "I've got a solid lead on the werewolf story."

His editor laughed.

"I mean it, Sandra. This is the real deal. I've found them. No question."

"*The real deal*," she scoffed. "Just like your story about monkeys hypnotizing the Supreme Court?"

"I still think you need to take that story seriously," said Dirk. "If you look at the court's recent track record for cases involving banana subsidies in South America—"

"Dirk, Dirk, Dirk. Save it," she said before settling into her desk. She took a drink of coffee. "This isn't *The New York Times*, this is *Really Real News*. You could write about Elvis eating Sasquatch sandwiches for all I care."

Her eyes widened. She grabbed a pencil.

"I like that," she said, scribbling down the idea while it was fresh. "Sasquatch sandwiches…."

"You might not care about the truth, but I do," interrupted Dirk. "Werewolves are real. They always have been. And they live in Canada."

"I humour you, Dirk, because you always make deadline and you generally spell English words correctly," said Sandra. "Why, pray tell, do the werewolves live in Canada?"

"I don't know. Maybe they like plaid shirts and ice hockey." He threw a jumbo box of dental floss into his bag. "All I know is that they're there, and I'm going to put them on the front page."

Dirk stuffed a few more items into his bag: a tube of toothpaste. A stapler. He moved a few items around to make room for a framed photo of the Loch Ness Monster. "You think I need the picture of Nessie?" he asked. "I'm running out of space."

Sandra hid her grin behind her coffee cup. She took a sip. "Oh, definitely," she said. "I never leave home without mine."

CHAPTER FOUR

MARCUS DOMINATED CONVERSATION OVER BREAK-fast. Kate's family sat in rapt attention. Marcus and John seemed to have lived their entire lives on the move.

"We would have stayed in Scotland forever," laughed Marcus. "That's where we're from…our people anyway. But there hasn't been a wolf in that country for three hundred years. Not that you'd know it by the fear and hatred of the people. One camper reported hearing us howling in the woods, and within a day, the papers were filled with letters to the editor demanding government action to protect the children." He leaned back. "I don't know about you, Brian, but I don't crave the flesh of children whether I'm wolf or human."

"Can't say that I do either," replied Brian. "But that doesn't erase centuries of fear. Irrational as it is, people are terrified of wolves. Always have been, probably always will be."

"Exactly," said Marcus. "And I fear an angry mob of wolf-haters more than they fear me. Our stay in Scotland was shorter than I had hoped."

"We've only moved a few times," said Lisa. "This place, we've lived here—what—maybe seven, eight years now?"

Brian nodded.

"You're lucky," said Marcus.

"Luck, and a low profile," said Brian. "We barely dared howl the first four or five summers we were here. Maybe we've become careless lately. You didn't seem to have much trouble finding us."

Marcus stared at him a moment with a blank expression. "Not too much, no."

"How did you know we weren't, you know, just regular wolves?" asked Brian.

Marcus shrugged. "There aren't any wolves around, far as I know. I mean, not for hundreds of years. I was pretty sure it was a safe bet you were like us."

Brian nodded.

"Have you met many other werewolves?" asked Lisa.

"Not many," said Marcus. "I don't think there are many of us left in the world. The few we have met don't even trust other werewolves. We've been asked to move along a couple of times. They were afraid too many of us in one spot would make people suspicious."

"I only ever met one other werewolf in my whole life before today," said Brian with a smirk, "and I married her."

Marcus smiled, but his eyes looked sad. "You were lucky. John's mum wasn't a wolf. It made things…" he searched for a word, "difficult."

"Where is she now?" asked Lisa.

Marcus looked at his hands. His demeanor darkened. "There was a fire," he said. "She didn't make it."

"Oh, how awful," said Lisa quickly. She touched her mouth.

"This was years ago," said Marcus, looking up into Lisa's eyes. "John doesn't even remember her."

"I'm so sorry," said Brian.

"Y'know," said Marcus with a short, bitter laugh, "she wasn't exactly thrilled when she found out the hairy truth about me." He glanced at his son. "It's been hard, just John and me, but it's been good, too.... I didn't know if he'd be a werewolf until his first full moon at thirteen." He sipped his tea. "But he heard the call. Not that he seems to care. Spends most full-moon nights curled up sleeping."

The group turned to look at John who was absently chewing a mouthful of bacon, oblivious to the conversation around him. He looked up. "What?" he said between bites.

Kate rolled her eyes and turned back to Marcus. "Does it happen like that for everyone? The call, I mean?" she asked.

"Seems to," replied Marcus. "Some wolves have a lot of funny theories and superstitions about where we come from, but that much seems to stay the same. We're all deaf to the call of the full moon until we're thirteen. They all describe it the same way: a low howl from the moon. Hear it, answer it, and you are a wolf."

"What if you don't answer it?" asked Kate.

Marcus shrugged. "I've never come across a were-wolf who hasn't. It's a powerful call. When you hear it, you'll know what I mean."

"But what if you don't?" said Kate. "What if you hear it, but just...don't answer?"

Marcus stared at her a moment. "Why don't you try it out tonight, birthday girl, and we'll know the answer?"

An uncomfortable silence hung over the group.

"What are you kids up to this morning?" asked Lisa, feigning a yawn and stretch.

"I was hoping to go to town," said Kate. She raised her eyebrows in hopeful anticipation.

Her parents looked at each other. Her father scowled slightly.

"Please?" Kate begged. "It's my birthday."

Brian turned to Marcus. "We try to keep a low profile. We only go into town for supplies a few times a year when we really need them."

"And nobody bothers you?" asked Marcus.

Brian grinned. "There's a rumour in town that we're deeply religious and will try to convert anyone who comes near our camp. People steer pretty clear," he said. "Right, kids?"

Bobby and Kate put their hands together in front of their chests as if they were deep in prayer. "Right, father," said Bobby before he burst out laughing.

"Seriously, though," said Kate. "Can I *please* go? I promise, I'll be good. Just to that restaurant at the motel for some fries or something."

"Well," said Lisa, trading a glance with Brian. "All right."

"John, why don't you tag along?" suggested Marcus.

John shrugged. "Okay."

"Can I come too?" implored Bobby.

"No," said Kate.

"Yes," corrected their mother.

"*Mum.*" Kate's eyes went wide.

"Of course you can go, dear. Don't spoil your lunch."

CHAPTER FIVE

DIRK SCANNED THE MENU AT THE GREASY DINER attached to his motel. Almost everything listed was offensive to his journalistic sensibilities. The gum-chewing waitress standing beside his table was growing impatient.

"Are you going to order or what?" she said between chomps.

"Just a second," said Dirk. "You don't seem to have a lot of options here."

"Why don't you just get the special?"

"What was that again?" he asked.

The woman rolled her eyes and repeated it for the third time.

"Two eggs any style, hash browns, toast, and coffee."

"Ha! What kind of fool do you take me for?"

The waitress looked around the room. "You really want me to answer that? What's wrong with eggs, hash browns, and toast?"

"For starters," said Dirk, getting excited, "eggs! Chicken eggs. As if we all don't know about the brain-controlling chemical the government infuses into the DNA of every yolk."

The waitress nearly swallowed her gum.

"Second," continued Dirk, "hash browns! Have you heard of a little thing called the MacNeil-Morton Report?"

The waitress shook her head.

"Didn't think so," said Dirk, nodding. "Let's just say your friendly local potato-grower has a few more ties to international terrorism than he'd lead you to believe. Third: toast—"

"Why don't you just get the oatmeal?" she asked.

Dirk scoffed. "Why don't you just pour me a bowl of rat poison?"

Give me a good reason not to, thought the waitress.

"Cottage cheese, then," she suggested.

Dirk thought a moment. "I could have cottage cheese."

"And, a fruit cup?" she asked.

Dirk paused. "Is there banana in the cup?"

"Do you *want* there to be banana in the cup?" she asked.

"I like banana very much," replied Dirk pleasantly. He handed her his menu.

"There," said the waitress. "That wasn't so hard. Can I pour you a cup of coffee?"

Dirk began to hyperventilate.

"Water it is," she said, walking toward the kitchen.

Two tables over, Kate and Bobby stared in silence as John dumped a fourth packet of sugar into his coffee.

"Are you going to *drink* that?" asked Kate.

John looked up. "I *like* coffee," he said.

"Right," she answered, rolling her eyes.

"What I don't get," said Bobby, "is why you would spend your *whole* full-moon night sleeping."

John shrugged. "I was tired," he said.

"But you only get one or two nights every month to be a wolf and go *crazy*!"

"Then I'll go crazy the next month," said John. "If I feel like it."

"Did you go crazy last month?" asked Bobby.

John thought. "Nope. Slept."

"And the month before that?"

John grinned. "Slept," he said.

"Have you ever done anything fun on a full moon?" implored Bobby.

"Sleeping can be fun," said John. "I just don't see what's so great about running around howling once a month."

Kate looked at him. Maybe this guy wasn't as dumb as she'd thought.

"You sound like Katie," said Bobby. "She wants to be a duck."

John arched his eyebrows. "Really?"

"Ha. Well...sure," said Kate. She blushed. "Why not?"

"That's cool," said John, nodding. "Werewolves in Central America tell stories of people who turn into all sorts of animals. In India, they talk about werecows, and Australian werewolves believe they're descendants of dingoes."

"Have you ever seen anyone turn into anything other than a wolf?" asked Kate.

"Nah," he replied, stirring his coffee. "Dad thinks it's all crap. People tell all sorts of weird stories. Still. It's interesting—" He stopped abruptly. He'd spotted something a few tables over.

"What?" asked Kate. "What is it?"

"That guy over there," whispered John. "The one with the bowl of cottage cheese. Recognize him?"

Kate and Bobby swivelled to look.

"Don't do that," hissed John. "He'll see you. Just be cool."

The brother and sister took turns peering at the man.

"Never seen him before," breathed Kate.

"Me neither," added Bobby. "Do you know him?"

"Maybe," whispered John. "He looks a bit different from his photo in the paper, but I think it's him."

"Who?" asked Kate.

"Let's just say, if it is who I think it is, we're kinda screwed," said John, stirring another packet of sugar into his coffee.

CHAPTER SIX

KATE, JOHN, AND BOBBY SAT ON A CONCRETE BUM-per in the motel parking lot.

"Don't you think we look just a little suspicious waiting out here for him like this?" asked Kate.

"Suspicious?" replied John. "We're teenagers. We loiter. It's what we do."

"Who is this guy, anyway?" asked Kate.

"'Dirt Bag,'" said John. "That's what my dad calls him. His real name is Dirk Bragg. Ever hear of the *Really Real News*?"

Kate and Bobby exchanged glances and shook their heads.

"It's one of those cruddy tabloids they sell in grocery stores with stories on the cover about alien abductions. They only sell it in the States. It's bad. Like, the lowest of the low. He writes for them."

"So, what's he doing here?" asked Kate.

"Good question. He could be chasing any story. But Dirt Bag's got a real thing for werewolves. As horrible as the *Really Real News* is, he's pretty good. The guy is relentless. I don't know how he does it, but he always seems to find us. We've had to move a bunch of times because of him. Dad *hates* him."

"You think he's here because of us?" asked Bobby.

"Could be. I'd like to find out for sure."

"How are you going to do that?" asked Kate.

The door to the diner opened before John could answer. Dirk walked out, crossed the parking lot to the door of a motel room, opened it with his key and entered.

"Now what?" asked Kate.

"Now, we wait for him to leave," replied John, nonchalantly. "Do you have a piece of paper and a pen?"

Kate rustled through her backpack and drew out a pad of paper and a stub of pencil.

"Thanks," said John. He flipped to an empty page and scribbled a few words.

Across the parking lot, Dirk re-emerged from his motel room. He climbed into an old white pickup truck and drove out of the lot.

John stood up and strode towards Dirk's room. Kate and Bobby scurried after.

"What are we doing?" asked Kate.

"We're going into his room to figure out why he's here," said John.

"For real?" asked Bobby. "Like, a break-in? Like we're spies or something? Cool!"

"Not *cool*," corrected Kate. "Illegal."

"*Illegal*," scoffed John. "I'm sure Dirt Bag has broken his fair share of laws to get a story. Besides, we're just grabbing something we left in his room."

"We didn't leave anything in his room!" said Kate. "I'm not doing this. No way."

They stood outside Dirk's door. Kate's hands were perched on her hips.

"Too bad," said John. A smile crept across his mouth. "How else are we going to get this back?"

He held up a piece of paper torn from Kate's notebook. Across it was scrawled:

> Katie Wereduck
>
> Come to the woods tonight and see for yourself, Dirt Bag!
>
> Quack, quack!

Kate lunged, but John stuffed the note into Dirk's mail slot before she could grab it.

"You moron!" she yelled.

"Maybe," shrugged John. "Want to help me get it back?"

Her eyes narrowed. Her nostrils flared.

"This is the coolest thing ever," said Bobby.

CHAPTER SEVEN

JOHN BOOSTED BOBBY INTO THE WINDOW BEHIND
Dirk's room, followed by Kate. Each grabbed one of
John's hands and pulled him into the room.

"I can't believe we're doing this," said Kate. "This
is stupid."

"Yeah," replied John. "But kinda stupid-fun,
right?"

"Right," said Bobby. He gave John a high-five.

"Morons," muttered Kate, crossing the room. She
picked up the note John had pushed through the mail
slot and stuffed it in her pocket.

"Okay. Let's go," she said.

"Not yet," said John. "Let's find out what he's
doing here."

Kate waited impatiently by the window as the boys
rummaged through the reporter's belongings. "Don't
make a mess, he'll know we were here," she said.

"How," said John, "could we possibly make this room any messier?"

Kate looked around the room. It was a disaster. She didn't know how long Dirt Bag had been staying here, but it had been long enough for him to cover the floor in crumpled heaps of clothing. Several blackened banana peels lay discarded on the desk. A pile of loose papers sat on the bed beside an expensive-looking camera and lens.

"What are those papers?" she asked.

John and Bobby moved to the bed and sorted through the pile.

"Even his handwriting is messy," said John. "None of this makes any sense. Wait—here's something…."

He held up a piece of paper and studied it carefully.

"What is it?" asked Kate.

"It's a list of phone numbers," said John. His eyes widened. "Whoa! My dad's cell number is here."

"Why would Dirt Bag have your dad's—"

Kate stopped mid-sentence. All three froze at the sound of a vehicle pulling into the parking spot just outside the room.

"He's back!" exclaimed Kate. "Let's go!"

Bobby ran to the back window, his eyes wild. Kate and John hoisted him by his legs. "It's a long way down!" he gasped.

"Just go!" hissed John.

Bobby toppled headfirst through the window. He tucked into a roll as he landed in the long grass below.

"You next," said John to Kate.

Before she could place her foot into his hands, they heard a key in the lock.

"Bathroom!" hissed John. "Shower!"

They rushed in, climbed into the tub, and drew the curtain closed just as the door opened.

"You are *such* a moron," whispered Kate.

CHAPTER EIGHT

SOMETHING WASN'T RIGHT.

As a reporter, Dirk had learned to trust his instincts. They'd kicked in as he drove his little pickup down the road, telling him to return to the motel.

He looked around the room. It was a mess. He made a mental note to keep things neater in the future so he could detect if someone had been searching through his stuff.

His notes lay jumbled on the bed where he'd left them. It was impossible to tell whether anyone had looked at them. Still, something was off.

He took two steps into the bathroom. On the other side of the shower curtain, Kate and John held their breath.

Dirk turned on the tap in the sink and let the water run warm before splashing some on his face. In the mirror, he could see the shower curtain closed behind him.

Dirk never left the shower curtain closed. Ever.

He knew exactly what was going on.

Kate heard the water being turned off, then the rattle of the towel on the rack as Dirk dried his face and hands.

Dirk stood perfectly still in the middle of the room for a long, agonizing moment. Kate was sure he was about to yank open the curtain. She squeezed John's hand. His fingertips turned purple.

Dirk walked out of the bathroom. He picked up the phone on the desk and dialled a familiar number.

"*Really Real News*," answered Dirk's editor.

"Sandra," he said. "It's me."

"Dirk! I didn't think I'd hear from you until tomorrow. What's up?"

"It's the werewolf story," he replied, glancing back to the bathroom. "We need to talk."

CHAPTER NINE

JOHN AND KATE STRAINED TO HEAR DIRK'S END of the conversation.

"Okay," said Sandra. She sounded concerned. "You don't normally check in like this. Everything all right?"

"Quite frankly, no," said Dirk. "Things aren't all right. The story is a *bust*. I thought I had a firm lead about werewolves in this area, but it turns out I was wrong."

Kate released a quiet sigh.

"There was definitely howling last night. The old farmer who told me about it was quaking in his pajamas. He thought the wolves were going to come tearing into his bedroom. It didn't take much snooping for me to find what was howling: a lonely German shepherd tied up at the farm next door."

"That's too bad, Dirk. I guess you'll have to make something up," said his editor. "It really isn't like you to check in like this. What's up?"

"Nothing is up," said Dirk clearly, enunciating every word. "But I am definitely packing up my things this morning, checking out of this motel, and heading back to New York."

"What's going on here, Dirk?" asked Sandra, sounding bothered. "I've never heard you give up this easy. Is something up?"

"Way, waaay up," said Dirk.

"Is someone listening to you right now?" she asked.

Dirk stared at the bathroom door. "Yes," he said.

A thousand kilometres away, Sandra sat bolt upright in her chair. "Are you safe?"

"Yes. I think so," he replied.

"Everything you just told me is bunk, isn't it?"

"Yes, it is," said Dirk.

"The person, or persons, listening in—are they werewolves?" asked Sandra.

"Yes," replied Dirk. "I'm sure of it."

CHAPTER TEN

KATE'S RELIEF AT AVOIDING THE FRONT PAGE OF *Really Real News* was quickly overshadowed by the fact that she was about to be discovered in the motel-room shower of its ace reporter.

"This is the worst birthday ever," she whispered to John.

John, who seemed to be enjoying himself, didn't even try to stifle a smile. They'd stood in the shower for close to twenty minutes, listening to Dirk toss clothes and papers into his bag.

"You know," whispered John, "sooner or later, this guy's going to have to take a pee, and I'm afraid I'm not going to be able to hold in my laughter when he does...."

"You," said Kate, "are a moron."

"You keep saying that," said John with a grin.

In the next room, Dirk attempted to close his over-stuffed duffle bag. He was sitting on it and tugging at the straps when a knock came to the door.

Dirk answered it to find the motel manager, Mr. Connors, standing next to a boy who looked to be about ten or eleven.

"Daddy!" yelled the boy as he leapt at Dirk and wrapped his arms around him.

Dirk did not hug back.

Bobby winced. The reporter stank of stale sausage and unwashed clothing.

"I'm sorry, there's been some mistake," said Dirk, looking helplessly at Mr. Connors. "I've never seen this boy in my life."

"*Daddy!*" yelled Bobby. "How can you *say* that? When are we going home?"

"Mr. Bragg," said Connors, glancing around and spotting Dirk's packed bag. "You need to clear this situation up. This boy here says you're his pappy, and by the looks of things, you're fixing to check out without him."

"But Mr. Connors, I assure you this is not my son. I don't even *have* a son."

Bobby started to cry. "Are you going to leave me here, Daddy?" He held his breath and lunged at him for a second hug. Dirk successfully deflected this attempt, holding the boy at arm's length.

"Bragg, I don't know what to say," said the motel manager. He lifted the battered ball cap from his head and scratched his scalp.

"The boy is lying," said Dirk firmly, his one hand still holding a flailing Bobby at bay.

"I'd like you to come down to the office so we can figure this out. I don't want to call the police unless I have to. Bad for business."

"Agreed," said Dirk, releasing Bobby. He stepped through the door and pulled it closed. "Let's go."

The two men led Bobby along the line of doors toward the motel office. He continued to shed tears like a baby while keeping a careful eye for any sign of John or his sister.

"Mummy's sure going...to b–be...mad when she...h–hears about this," he gasped between sobs.

"I'll give you this, kid. You put on a good show," said Dirk. "Connors, are you sure this isn't some local kid? You don't recognize him at all?"

The motel manager stopped and took a good look at Bobby. "These kids all look the same to me," he said. "We get so many people coming in and out, I hardly remember faces. Still," he said folding his arms, "he looks a bit familiar."

"Yes?" prompted Dirk.

"Y'ain't one of them religious folks with the camp out by that little lake, are ya?" He snapped his fingers a few times, trying to jog his memory. "What's yer daddy's name?"

Bobby's heart raced. Drawing attention to his family was the last thing he needed. He looked at the ground. "I don't...know what you're t–talking about. *This*...is my daddy," he said, pointing at Dirk.

A small movement behind the backs of the men caught Bobby's attention. A hand snuck around the corner at the far end of the motel. It flashed an unmistakable thumbs-up sign.

"Y'know," said Bobby, wiping away his tears. "Maybe I'm wrong." He took a good look at Dirk. "Oh, silly me. I *am* wrong. You're not my daddy. *Bye!*"

Bobby dashed off before Dirk or Connors could say a word. As he raced around the corner of the building, John and Kate grabbed him and pulled him into the woods.

"That was *awesome!*" yelled John as he dodged between spruce trees.

"*Daddy!*" mimicked Bobby, squealing with laughter. "You should have seen his face!"

"You are *both* morons," said Kate between breaths. Her face beamed, in spite of herself. "Especially you," she gasped, punching John in the arm.

CHAPTER ELEVEN

"DAMN IT!" YELLED MARCUS. THE SCORCHING handle of the teakettle stung the flesh of his palm. He threw it to the ground, its steaming contents spilling out onto the grass.

"I should have warned you," said Marge, walking around the corner of the cabin with an armload of firewood. "The kettle gets a bit hot."

Marcus waved his hand in the air.

"I could have seriously burned myself," he said.

Marge put down the wood and picked up the kettle. She gave it a shake. "There's a bit left in here. Still want some?"

Marcus gaped at the older woman as she held the hot metal in her hand. She grinned.

"I must have thick skin. Care for a cup?"

"Sure," he replied, holding out his mug. "Lisa and Brian still asleep?"

"I don't expect them up for hours," she replied, pouring the last few drops of tea into Marcus's cup. "You certainly didn't sleep long."

"I've never been able to sleep during the day. Funny problem for a nocturnal animal, wouldn't you say?"

Marge nodded.

Marcus had barely taken his first sip when the phone in his pocket began to ring. He put down his mug and fished it out.

"Yeah," he answered. "Oh, hi. Where are you?"

He listened a moment. "*What?*" he sputtered into the phone. He seemed agitated. He turned his body away from the fire before speaking again, this time more quietly. "Did they know who you were?"

Another pause. "Well, that's a relief," he looked over his shoulder at Marge. "Look, this really isn't the best time. I'll talk to you later. Right. Bye."

He turned off his phone and slipped it back into his pocket.

"Friend of yours?" asked Marge.

Marcus took a sip of tea. "An old acquaintance."

Marge began stacking firewood. "Quite a coincidence, you running into Lisa and Brian last night," she said.

"Quite," said Marcus.

"What are the chances of two sets of werewolves finding each other in the backwoods of Charlotte County like that?"

"Couldn't say," said Marcus. "But, if you figure we all came here looking for the same thing—a quiet spot away from people—it's not so hard to believe."

"I suppose," said Marge. "How long did you say you were planning on staying around here?"

"I didn't," said Marcus, his grey eyes unblinking.

"I haven't figured you out yet, Marcus, but I don't believe you are what you seem," said Marge. She sat down across the fire from him.

"No," he said, blowing on his tea. "But few of us are, Grandmother Wolf."

CHAPTER TWELVE

"ONE, TWO, THREE!" YELLED BOBBY AS HE LEAPT from a rocky ledge above the lake. The wind whistled through his ears and hair as he swung out on a rope tied to an overhanging branch. He flew toward the surface of the water before his momentum picked back up and swung him high over the centre of the lake. He released the rope and fell, laughing and splashing into the clear blue water.

"Did you see me?" he sputtered as he breached the surface. "Did you *see* me?"

"Yes, but we saw you the first hundred times, too," said Kate absently without looking up from her book. She lay stretched out on a blanket, her head resting on her backpack. John sat close by, breaking pieces from his sandwich and tossing them to a noisy flock of birds.

Kate's eyes drifted from her book to John. He was trying to feed a group of ducks, but a bunch of hungry gulls was beating them to the prize. Each time a chunk of bread landed within reach of a duck, an obnoxious gull dashed at it, gobbling it down in one gulp.

"C'mon, duckies. You've got to work harder than that," said John.

"Ducks are too cool to make a scene over a chunk of bread," said Kate. "The gulls look stupid splashing around like that."

"One, two, *three!*" came Bobby's voice from across the lake.

Splash!

"Did you see me?" sputtered Bobby.

"Bobby illustrates my point exactly," said Kate.

John sniffed a laugh through his nose. He tore off another chunk of his sandwich and threw it to the birds.

Kate pretended to turn her attention to her book, *Just Ducky: Everything You Ever Wanted to Know About Our Web-Footed Friends.* Really, she was holding a lingering glance at John, who was conveniently distracted by the birds.

She had to admit it: he was cute.

Just be cool, thought Kate. She searched for something interesting in her book to talk about.

"Did you know some species of duck mate for life?" she blurted.

That was dumb.

"Really?" said John, genuinely interested. "I was just thinking *that* duck and *that* duck seemed to be a thing," he said, pointing in turn to a mottled-brown female and a green-headed male. "Before I started throwing bread, they seemed to be doing *couple* things:

swimming together, bobbing for food. But then, *this* chick came in," he pointed to a second female, larger than the first, "and the guy was like, 'whoa, who is *this?*'"

"The poor duck," said Kate, watching the smaller female swim at the edges of the group. "She looks lonely."

John looked at Kate. Their eyes met. *He's not looking away,* she thought. She bit at her lower lip.

"Guys!" Bobby announced as he waded through the water toward them. The group of ducks and gulls broke apart.

"Hey, Bobby." said John, turning away from Kate. "Did you know some ducks mate for life?"

"Huh," said Bobby, unimpressed. "Did you know wolves *eat* ducks?"

Kate grumbled and turned back to her book.

"What? It's true," said Bobby. "If you were a duck and I was a wolf, I'd have no choice but to eat you. I wouldn't even have to apologize. It would be my *nature.*"

Bobby howled and lunged at a pair of ducks who had strayed too close.

"That's bull," said John.

Bobby stopped splashing.

"What?" he asked.

"Some werewolves make a big deal of the crazy urges we feel. That we *yearn* to take down a deer, or can't *stop* ourselves from chasing rabbits." He threw another chunk of sandwich. "Bull."

"Really?" asked Kate. She put her book aside and sat up.

"Really," said John. "When I'm a wolf, I'm still me. With fur."

Bobby furrowed his brow. "But, I kind of want to chase rabbits and stuff."

"Then chase rabbits!" said John. "But don't blame it on being a wolf. Sounds to me like you just like chasing rabbits." He smirked. "Hurray, a hobby! Go find a rabbit to chase. You'll love it."

John plunked beside Kate and smiled at her. A tiny flock of ducks took off in her stomach. She leaned her shoulder into his.

The sound of wheels on gravel drew their attention to the camp's driveway. A beat-up yellow station wagon pulled in and parked beside the cabin. A dark-haired woman in cutoff shorts and a grey tank top emerged from the driver's seat. She pulled a pair of oversized sunglasses from her face and scanned the camp. She spotted the group by the lake and gave a friendly wave.

"Katie! Bobby! Hi!" she shouted. She walked toward them.

"Aunt Bea!" replied Bobby. He ran toward her and wrapped her in a dripping-wet hug.

"Who," whispered John with big lusty eyes, "is that?"

Kate's eyes narrowed. Her heart fell to her stomach. She waved to her carefree, intelligent, and beautiful aunt.

"It's my Aunt Beatrice," said Kate. "Aunt Bea."

"*Wow*," gasped John.

Kate felt like a small brown duck swimming around the edge of a pond.

CHAPTER THIRTEEN

LAUGHTER DRIFTED LIKE SMOKE ABOVE THE campfire. Empty plates, dirty with the crumbs from Kate's birthday cake, lay scattered about.

"Fabulous cake, Mum," said Bea. She licked the last bit of frosting from her fork. "How you manage to bake a cake like that over the coals of a fire, I'll never know."

Marge winked. "Slather enough icing on anything and it'll taste all right."

"Hear! Hear!" said Brian.

The sky was clear. The moon was rising. Everyone was in a fabulous mood. Everyone except for Kate. She tried to join in the excitement, but she felt none of it. Just the dull ache of a girl watching the boy she likes fawn over someone else.

John sat next to Bea. He peppered her with questions. He laughed too hard at her jokes. The fact that Aunt Bea was oblivious to John's gushing only seemed to egg him on.

Kate looked at the meagre pile of gifts that sat beside her. Her family had a rule about birthday presents: they had to be homemade. This saved them from making needless trips to town, with the side-benefit being gifts that were more personal, more thoughtful.

Her mother had bound pages together into a small book and written in it some of her own favourite poems.

Her dad had attempted to knit her a scarf. "It's not quite done," he said sheepishly as she unwrapped the tangle of red wool.

"I love it, Dad. Thanks."

He brightened. "I'll finish it before it gets cold this fall. I promise."

Bobby's present looked like a stack of pine cones held together by sap.

"It's modern art," he announced.

Her grandmother gave her a card made from heavy, cream-coloured paper. Inside, she'd sketched a duck tucked into a nest of reeds. Beneath the picture read the caption *Quiet Dignity*.

Kate looked up at her grandmother and smiled.

"So, are you ready for tonight, or what?" asked Bea, pulling Kate back from her thoughts.

"I guess," Kate shrugged.

"You better be. I drove two whole days to be here for your first wolf night," she said. "Where are we going to do this?" she asked, looking at Brian.

"About a ten-minute hike up that way," he said, pointing north. "There's a small clearing on a bit of a hill with a full view of the southern sky. A nice spot to see the moon."

"Sounds perfect," said Bea. She beamed at Kate. "This is going to be a blast."

Kate smiled. She really wanted it to be. A big part of her wanted to be excited about being a wolf, to feel like she belonged.

"Oh, John," she said, remembering something. "Were you going to tell your dad about that Dirt Bag guy?"

John shot her an urgent look that could only mean *shut up*. Her eyebrows furrowed in confusion.

Marcus nearly spit out his tea. "What?" he said, looking at John. "Dirt Bag? Are you sure?"

John nodded.

Marcus cursed beneath his breath. "And were you planning to tell me?"

"I didn't…think," began John sheepishly.

"Who's Dirt Bag?" interrupted Lisa.

"*Dirk Bragg*," explained Marcus. His face was grim. "A reporter with a trashy tabloid called *Really Real News*."

"Do you think he's here because of us?" asked Lisa.

"Well, he's their self-appointed werewolf reporter, so, good guess," said Marcus.

"I don't think we need to worry about him," said Kate, trying to sound casual. "He was leaving town. He said the locals here put him on a wild goose chase about werewolves."

"Well, that's good to hear," said Marcus, still seeming uneasy. "How did you hear that?"

John and Kate looked at each other. Their minds raced to find a way to tell the story without mentioning that they'd broken into his motel room.

"He was at the table next to us at the diner," sputtered John. "We heard him talking on his cell phone. He left town in his truck after that."

"That's not how it happened," said Bobby. "I thought you guys said you heard him when you were in his—"

Kate clamped a hand over Bobby's mouth. "Yeah, Bobby's a bit confused because he was in the bathroom when we heard him," said Kate. She looked her brother in the eye. "Right, Bobby?"

Bobby mumbled something under her hand. She removed it.

"Right," he said. "Bathroom."

"Even so," said Lisa, "I don't want to take any chances tonight."

"Me neither," said Brian looking at his watch. "We'll have to have a good look around the woods tonight before we head to the clearing. The last thing we need is a reporter snooping around."

"But he said he was going home," argued Kate.

"Better to be safe. And we'll have to keep quiet tonight in the woods. One howl each, to transform, but after that, we'd better keep our voices down."

"No howling?" asked Bobby. He looked dejected.

"You're not even a wolf yet, Bobby. What's the problem?" asked Kate.

He shrugged. "I *like* the howling."

"You won't miss it," said Marge. "You need to stay in the cabin tonight."

"But Grandma!"

"No buts," she said.

Bobby deflated.

Kate looked at Marcus. He wore a serious face. And he was staring at her father.

"Brian," he said. "What would you do if you ran across Dirt Bag tonight in the woods?"

"I don't know," replied Brian. "Probably duck behind a bush and hope he hadn't seen me. And start packing. There's no way we can stay if he knows we're here."

Marcus shook his head. "I've done that too many times," he said.

"What else *could* you do?" asked Bea. "He puts us in his paper and *someone* is going to believe him. The more people who believe, the less likely we'll be able to live in any sort of peace."

"I think I'd sleep a lot easier at night if he wasn't around to tell anyone about me," said Marcus. The whole group went silent.

"What are you suggesting?" asked Lisa.

"I'm not suggesting anything," said Marcus. He stood up and dumped the dregs of his tea into the fire. "I'd just like some of that peace Bea was talking about."

He turned and walked away.

CHAPTER FOURTEEN

THE SOUND OF BREAKING GLASS ECHOED THROUGH
the old, empty house. A hand reached through the
newly broken windowpane in the door and felt around
blindly for the deadbolt. When it found what it was
searching for it snapped open the lock.

Bits of broken glass crunched beneath Dirk's feet
as he walked into the house. He looked around. Dusty
strips of floral wallpaper hung in the hallway. An old
wooden table, its top stained with a mixture of age and
whatever had been dripping from the ceiling, was the
only piece of furniture in the kitchen.

Dirk stood in the middle of the kitchen and
turned slowly around. A thick layer of dust covered the
checkered linoleum floor. The refrigerator's rounded
corners—which must have, decades ago, given it a
futuristic look—screamed *1950s décor*. Dirk approached
a calendar on the wall. The date on the page locked

the entire house in April of 1983. This place had been empty a long time.

"Perfect," said Dirk, dropping his bag in the corner.

The old house was just what he needed. He'd been looking for an empty spot to set up in: a house whose owners had long abandoned this part of the country in search of jobs further west. When he'd spotted the moss-covered rooftop peeking through the trees along the road as he drove around the area, it seemed too good to be true. But it was clear now that no one had set foot in the house for years. That, and it was only about a kilometre from the werewolves' camp.

He rummaged through the house for supplies. In a drawer in the old parlour he discovered most of an old candle. He stuck the butt-end into an empty bottle he'd found in one of the bedrooms and lit the wick. He placed it on the kitchen table; its warm flickering light filled the growing darkness of the room.

Dirk sat on the wooden crate that he'd dragged into the kitchen to use as a chair and began to peel a banana. Through the window over the sink, he could see the sun hanging low in the sky.

He'd been careless that morning. It was his own fault he'd been discovered by those kids. He would have to pay for his carelessness with patience: a whole month's worth. But the story of a lifetime was within his reach. It was worth waiting until the next full moon.

Across the room on the countertop, he spotted a mouse. It chattered and waved its front paws at him, scolding Dirk for invading its space.

Dirk took a bite of banana. "Home sweet home."

CHAPTER FIFTEEN

KATE DREW FURTHER INTO HERSELF AS SUNSET approached. She didn't feel right. This was her wolf night, she was supposed to feel—how was she supposed to feel? She looked at the faces of her family. They were becoming giddy and animated as the evening wore on, like the coming night was some sort of drug.

Kate didn't feel those things.

She stole away from the fire to spend a few minutes alone in the forest before she began her new life as a werewolf. A burst of laughter from the group followed her into the canopy of the woods.

That's what I'm going to be, thought Kate. *What's wrong with that?*

Everything seemed wrong with it.

It was like growing up in a family of plumbers, and being told your whole life that when you grow up, you have to be a plumber too.

Maybe she didn't want to be a plumber. Maybe she wanted to be a carpenter. Or a used-car salesman. Or a sheep farmer. Or a ballpoint pen repairman. Anything but a plumber.

It just would have been nice to be asked what *she* wanted to be.

Kate sat on the trunk of a fallen tree and tried to decide if it was worth crying. It probably was, but she couldn't find any tears.

Being twelve sucks, she thought.

She remembered it was her birthday.

Being thirteen sucks, too.

"I thought I saw you sneak off in this direction," came her grandmother's voice from just up the trail. Marge strode into view. "Mind if I join you?"

"It's a free forest," said Kate, moving over to make room on the trunk. "Thanks for the card, Grandma. It was really beautiful."

"It was just a small thing," said her grandmother, dismissing her with a gentle wave of her hand.

They sat a few minutes in silence. Kate thought about how that made her grandmother so great. There are lots of people who are good company when you're talking. There are very few who are good company when you're not talking.

"So you don't want to be a wolf," said Marge finally, as if picking up a conversation they were already having.

"I really don't," said Kate. "And it's not like I haven't tried. I just don't. And I hate that I don't have any choice about it."

Marge nodded. "It's not an easy life," she said. "Your grandfather never liked it much."

"Really?" Kate was startled. She couldn't remember her grandfather, but she'd always assumed he was just as enthusiastic about being a wolf as the rest of her family.

"He never looked forward to a full moon the way your mum and dad do, or the way I do." She smiled. "I really enjoy it. I feel like we're all our true selves when we're wolves."

"Even the howling?"

"*Even* the howling," she said. "I like how we treat each other when we're wolves."

"Like wrestling and biting each others' ears?" asked Kate.

"Some of that, yes," she said. Marge's smile extended to her eyes. "But we're a lot more affectionate when we're wolves, aren't we? Humans have wonderful words to tell each other how we feel, but we don't often use them. Wolves don't have words. So we touch noses. We nip playfully. We howl in joy."

Kate stared into the trees.

"I know you don't think you'll like it," continued Marge, sliding off the tree trunk. "But tonight, when you become a wolf, I think you'll discover a voice you didn't know you had. When you do, come find me. We'll talk like wolves."

Kate's grandmother turned and walked back up the trail towards camp.

Kate finally found her tears, but she wasn't sad.

CHAPTER SIXTEEN

KATE WALKED SLOWLY THROUGH THE WOODS TO the clearing. She could only just see the sky through the trees, but she knew sundown would be soon. From somewhere overhead, she heard the whistling of wind through wings. She looked up and saw the silhouette of a pair of ducks passing overhead. It was too dark to tell what kind.

Kate knew her family expected her to show up in the clearing as mopey as she'd been that afternoon. Kate: The Reluctant Werewolf. Kate: The Heartbroken Teenager.

That wasn't who she wanted to be. That wasn't how she wanted to be seen.

Kate forced a smile onto her lips and made up her mind.

"I *am* a werewolf," she whispered.

She decided she would walk into that clearing as a confident teenager. She would hug her parents, her aunt, and her grandmother. She might even be polite to John. Teenage boys were stupid anyway.

She paused at the edge of the clearing, straightened her posture, took a deep breath, and strode in. As she entered, the heavy forest air became cool and refreshing.

Her family stood waiting. She hugged her mum first.

"Are you ready?" asked Lisa.

"Of course," she replied. "I love you, Mum."

She hugged her father.

"I'm so proud of you," he said.

"For turning thirteen?" said Kate dryly. "Yeah, that was tough."

She hugged her grandmother.

"My beautiful girl," said Marge, smoothing her hair.

She hugged her aunt.

"Are you excited?" asked Bea.

Kate's face beamed. "Definitely."

"Sun's going down," said Marcus striding into the clearing. Beside him walked John.

"Hey. I've decided I may not nap *all* night," said John. "It being a special occasion and all."

"Big of you," she replied, not looking him in the eye.

"We've only got a minute," said Bea. "Kate, it's *your* wolf night. I think you should be the first to answer the call."

"I like it," nodded Brian. He reached his hand out to his daughter. "Come stand with us."

Kate stood arm-in-arm with her parents, feeling the last rays of the setting sun on her face. She looked briefly to the cold white face of the moon. Something fluttered in her stomach.

The colour of the western sky faded from deep orange to red to pink as the sun slipped below the trees. When it finally disappeared, they all turned to face the moon. All was silent for a moment as they waited for the call.

"*Whooooo*," came a low voice through the still night air. It seemed to echo from the trees, the earth, the sky.

"There it is," said Lisa, squeezing her daughter's shoulder. "Can you hear it?"

Kate nodded.

"*Whooooo*," came the call again.

"Are you going to answer it, or what?" said John.

"You're being called, Kate," said her father. "You'd better answer."

There was something in that call. A tone Kate didn't expect.

"*Whooooo*."

"Answer it," said Marcus firmly.

Kate's eyes darted from Marcus to John to her parents. The pressure of being told who to be was stronger than ever.

"*Whooooo*."

The confidence she'd felt moments earlier was fading. This wasn't right. *She* was in charge of her life. Not her parents. Not Marcus. Not John.

But that voice made her feel different. It sounded— she wasn't sure what it sounded like, but it didn't make her feel pressured to become anything. It wasn't telling her who to be.

"*Whooooo?*"

It was asking.

It was asking her *who* she was and *who* she wanted to be.

She knew exactly who she was. She had always known. And here she was, finally being asked.

"*Quack*," she replied quietly.

Then, with a new confidence she'd never felt before: "*Quack! Quack! Quack!*"

CHAPTER SEVENTEEN

KATE FELT A CHILL RIPPLE THROUGH HER FLESH as her entire body broke out in goose pimples; each gave birth to a tiny brown feather. She could feel her body becoming smaller and lighter.

She ran her tongue along her teeth to find they were being sucked into her gums. Her lips and nose stretched in front of her face—the skin becoming tough and yellow.

She held her hands before her and watched as the fingers on each hand melded into a single point. Her arms flopped and turned at awkward angles before folding neatly upon her back.

Her legs shrank and became as skinny as twigs. The skin between her toes stretched and pulled until she had two perfect webbed feet.

She looked up and saw six pairs of eyes staring at her in disbelief.

"*Quack?*" she said.

Kate was a duck. A beautiful, if unassuming, brown mallard.

Her family was so transfixed by what had happened, they had forgotten to answer the call themselves. Bea remembered first.

"Way to go, Katie!" she cried. "*Ah-wooooo!*"

The others joined in the howl and began their own transformations. Not that Kate stuck around to watch.

She only questioned for a moment whether she'd be able to figure out the mechanics of flying. She stretched her wings, took a few rapid steps, and flapped herself into the air.

Kate flew straight over the heads of her family as they changed from human to wolf form. Gaining altitude, she skimmed the tops of the trees at the fringe of the clearing. She leaned to the right, making a wide sweeping arc, flying higher with every beat of her wings.

"I'm flying!" she tried to yell. "Mum! Dad! It's me! *Flying!*"

The only sound that came from her bill was a series of excited quacks.

She flapped harder. She loved the feel of the cool night air through her feathers: the quiet whistling of her wings as they carried her fast and far.

Flying over the camp, from this height, her home and belongings looked strange and unfamiliar—like scenery in a model train yard. She flew over the forest, noting the textures and smells of the different trees as she whizzed just above the canopy. She soared over the river, watching its water gush and flow over the contours of the land as it rolled slowly toward the sea.

She turned back toward camp. As the lake came into view, she flew lower. Her wings filled with air like feathered parachutes as she glided the last dozen metres to the water. She stretched her feet before her like a pair of webbed pontoons.

Kate skied briefly on the surface of the water before she lost her momentum, then bobbed mid-lake, her wings folded gracefully across her back.

I am a duck, she thought. *I don't know how it happened, but I am a duck.*

As the joy of a thousand Christmas mornings settled in her stomach, she knew exactly what she needed to do next. She paddled toward shore and waddled up onto the beach.

She began to shake her rear end. Slowly at first, then faster. Her tail feathers sprayed water about her as they made the *whap, whap, whap* sound she'd admired so many times before.

She'd waited her whole life for this moment.

CHAPTER EIGHTEEN

KATE WADED BACK INTO THE WATER AND MADE slow circles in the lake. She dipped her face into the water and felt her backside tip into the air. Her bill sucked and filtered tiny bits of green plants and goo from the water that she had seen the ducks on the lake feeding on before. She came back up for air, and swallowed.

Interesting texture, she thought, smacking her bill to examine the flavour. *Must be an acquired taste.*

Something was rustling the long grass across the lake from Kate. Out stepped a gangly wolf with reddish-brown fur. Wolf or not, Kate would recognize John anywhere.

With his front legs stretched before him, he lowered his head and wagged his tail high in the air. He looked less like a wolf and more like a dog asking to play a game of fetch.

Kate quacked a few times just to prove she could. She paddled in circles, pretending she wasn't bothered by John's presence. He whined.

With slow kicks of her webbed feet, she swam toward him. John cocked his head to one side as she closed the gap between them. Kate held his gaze as she inched closer. His tail gave an involuntary wag as her face approached his.

Peck!

Kate drove her bill into the bridge of John's nose. As he drew back in shock, she turned and kicked a small wave of water in his face.

He stepped into the lake, and swatted at the water with his paw in a futile attempt to splash her back. She made a second approach, readying her bill to strike again. He was, after all, on her turf.

John knew when to quit. He retreated to the long grass.

Kate dipped her head into the water and sifted for more of the green goo. It didn't taste so bad once you got used to it.

CHAPTER NINETEEN

KATE TURNED TO FACE THE WIDE EXPANSE OF water.

Okay, she thought. *You can do this.*

She didn't fancy the idea of John seeing her crash into the reeds on her very first water takeoff, but she sighed a long whistling breath and started paddling her feet. She extended her wings as she gathered speed. As her body rose out of the water, she pulled up her feet.

Flawless, she thought, soaring over John's head.

The camp lake was connected by river to a series of several smaller lakes. Flying north, Kate had only a few hundred metres to go before she'd come upon another lake. *Bingo.* She spotted about a dozen ducks sleeping in the shadows of the willow trees along the shore—likely the same ducks John had tossed bits of sandwich to earlier.

Kate touched down on the lake and glided to a stop. She kept her distance from the ducks. She didn't know whether they'd take kindly to a new female hanging around their flock.

She paddled idly, mid-lake, trying to look cool: dabbling in the water, filtering bits of grass into her bill. Her third mouthful turned up a wriggling bug. Gagging on a water beetle didn't strike her as the sort of thing a cool duck did to win friends. She swallowed it whole.

Not bad.

The other ducks had certainly noticed her arrival. A dozen pairs of eyes followed her as she swam and dabbled.

Kate wondered if ducks have small talk, and how she might go about saying, "Hey, nice lake you've got here."

"*Quack?*" was all she could muster.

A few of the ducks quacked in response. The largest male in the group waddled into the lake. The rest followed. They swam in formation like a navy flotilla intercepting an unknown ship.

Why am I so nervous? thought Kate as they approached. *They're just ducks.* Butterflies fluttered in her tiny tummy.

The ducks bore down on her in the darkness with the big male in front. A wake of ripples streamed behind him like a large V.

"*Quack!*" said Kate as they came nearer. "*Quack, quack!*"

Maybe she appeared too eager. Maybe she hadn't hit the level of cool she had been shooting for.

The ducks just sailed past as if she wasn't there. They didn't even look at her.

"*Quack*," she repeated as the last duck swam past. The butterflies turned to stone and rested heavily in her gut.

The flock picked up speed and took off. They circled the lake once and flew north.

Rejected, she thought, *by ducks*.

She looked down at the water, resting her bill and chin on her breast. She felt very alone.

"*Wacka*," came a voice.

Kate looked up.

"*Wacka*." A small brown duck eyed her curiously.

Kate must have missed this little female. Kate wondered if this was the same little duck that had been snubbed earlier by the big male.

"*Quack?*" said Kate.

"*Wacka*," replied the duck, nodding slightly.

Kate had no idea what she and this duck had said to each other, but she was pretty sure she'd just made her first duck-friend.

CHAPTER TWENTY

DIRK SQUINTED THROUGH THE LAST BIT OF LIGHT of the flickering candle on the table. An unfinished game of solitaire sat on the table before him.

"A black three…" he said just below his breath. "Three, three, three, three…."

He scanned the stack of cards for the fifth time. There had to be a black three somewhere. He went back to the remaining cards in his hand. It was cheating to dip into the deck like this, but Dirk wasn't above that.

"Three, three, three, three…" he hummed. "Damn."

He dropped the cards on the table and shuffled them into a pile. He considered dealing another game, but he'd already played seventeen rounds and lost twelve.

His candle had just a few minutes left before it would burn itself out. He blew it out in case he needed it in the night.

Dirk pushed back his chair and walked to the front door. A chorus of crickets announcing the arrival of late summer greeted him as he stepped into the cool night air. He closed his eyes and took a deep breath.

Today hadn't gone well, but he was so close to something great he could feel it. He'd chased down many false leads before, but this was the real thing. Earlier tonight, just after the sun had gone down, he'd *heard* them. Wolves were howling in a place where they've been extinct for more than a hundred years.

Yes, he could wait here for a month. He'd talk to Sandra tomorrow. She'd understand. She always understood when there was promise of a juicy story.

A faint sound drifted from the woods. As it became louder, he recognized the individual *quacks* from a flock of ducks in flight. They passed over the house, flying north.

Dirk looked at his watch. *Why would ducks be awake so late?*

He got up and walked back into the house and crashed on the musty living room couch.

Probably afraid of the wolves, he thought as he drifted off to sleep.

CHAPTER TWENTY-ONE

A SMALL FEMALE DUCK WADDLED ALONG A SUNNY dirt path. It looked up and saw the noon sun shining through a few passing clouds.

The duck proceeded on its path towards the giant box where the people lived. As she approached, she saw the door swing open and close. The banging sound as it shut gave her a start, but she bravely continued her approach and announced her arrival.

"*Wacka*," said the duck.

Marge looked down at the sound. A large grin spread across her face. "Katie," she called, her eyes not leaving the duck. "I think you have a visitor."

A muffled response came from inside the cabin. Kate emerged rubbing her eyes. "A what?" she said, looking exhausted. "Who's here, Grandma?"

Marge nodded in the direction of the duck.

"*Wacka*," said the duck.

Kate brightened. "Wacka! It's you! Hi, Wacka!" She crouched on her knees and greeted the duck with a pat on her head. "How are you doing, sweetie?"

"*Wacka*," repeated the duck.

"Did you come looking for me? Oh, what a smart duck…" gushed Kate.

"Aren't you going to introduce us?" asked Marge.

"Oh, Grandma," said Kate. "This is Wacka. We met last night. Isn't she gorgeous?"

Marge smiled. "Stunning," she said. "Do you suppose she'd like a crust of bread?"

"I'm sure she would."

Kate sat with Wacka on her lap, feeding her bits of bread and stroking her feathery back.

"And what about you?" asked Marge. "Can I get you some lunch? I imagine flying and swimming work up an appetite."

"Would you?" asked Kate. "I'm *starving*."

"Sure. But you've got to tell me everything about last night."

"It was so fantastic, Grandma!" exclaimed Kate. "It was just—" She searched for the right word. "Perfect." Kate talked on as Marge fueled with her sandwiches and cups of tea.

"And you *enjoyed* the goo, did you?" interjected Marge at one point in the story.

"I wouldn't say '*enjoyed*' is the right word," said Kate. "But…."

Marge laughed. Kate kept on, repeating whole sections of her story as more members of her family emerged from the cabin.

"Kate, you are the cutest duck," laughed her aunt. "Not everyone can wear feathers, but *my* girl, you work them."

"Hey, what became of you last night, Bea?" asked Lisa. "One minute you were with us, the next you were gone. Where'd you go?"

Bea blushed. "Oh, I was around."

"Around where?" teased Brian.

"Oh, you know," stammered Bea. She looked more than relieved to find a distraction from the conversation as she spotted Marcus striding into the campfire clearing.

"Good morning," said Marcus. He settled in close beside Bea on the bench. Kate thought he looked awfully comfortable at her side, and Bea didn't seem to mind.

"Well, let's get down to it, then," said Brian, clearing his throat. "What happened last night? How did a werewolf end up turning into a duck?"

All eyes turned to Kate.

"Don't look at me," she said. "I just quacked."

"It's amazing," said Lisa. "I've never seen or heard of anything like it."

"Me neither," said Marcus.

"Have you ever heard of something like this, Mum?" asked Lisa.

"No," said Marge. She paused and pursed her lips. "Maybe."

"Another wereduck?" asked Kate.

"No, definitely not that," said Marge thoughtfully. "But your grandfather told me a story once. It was a story his mother told him, and her mother told her."

The group fell quiet as Marge started her story.

"There was a pair of sisters. Their mum was a wolf; their dad was not. When they were kids, no one was sure if they'd become wolves at all."

Marge watched the fire as she spoke.

"The older sister became a wolf, which was a relief to them all. As the younger girl got closer to thirteen, she became terrified that it wouldn't happen. She just didn't feel the wolf in her like her sister did. She was afraid her family would send her away if she didn't become a wolf. One day, after a rain, she went looking in the woods for a set of wolf tracks."

"Wolf tracks?" said Brian.

"I've heard of that," said Marcus. "Drinking water from the footprint of a wolf is said to turn you into a werewolf. That's a northern European legend."

"Well, she found footprints all right," added Marge, "and she drank the muddy water."

"Gross," said Bobby.

"When the full moon came," Marge continued, ignoring Bobby, "instead of howling, the girl started making an odd sound. Like yipping or yelping."

"What happened?" asked Kate.

"She turned into a fox," said Marge. "A red fox. As soon as she grew her red coat and black socks she scurried off into the woods. They never saw her again."

Marge picked up a stick and poked at the coals in the fire pit. "I always thought it was just a story, but there it is."

"Well," said Marcus, "legends usually begin with a piece of truth. I don't think Ducky here has been sipping from any webbed footprints. Have you?"

Kate shook her head.

"But if the girl in the story didn't feel like she was a wolf," continued Marcus, "maybe she was meant to be something else. And maybe we're looking at the same thing right here."

He nodded to Kate.

"So, does this mean any of us can turn into whatever we want?" asked Bea.

"Who can say?" said Brian. "I still feel like a wolf."

"Me too," said Marcus.

The discussion continued. A yawning figure emerged from the woods and approached the fire. John ran a hand thought his messy hair. He had obviously just woken up.

"What's going on?" he asked, stretching.

"Just trying to figure out our little duck mystery," said Marcus. "What'd you get up to last night?"

John rubbed a tender spot on the bridge of his nose. "I got attacked by a duck," he said.

"Kate!" exclaimed her mother.

"She was just playing," said John with a grin. "But *that* was so much fun that I decided to sleep the rest of the night."

"Again?" exclaimed Bobby.

John shrugged. He plopped on the ground next to Kate and Wacka.

"Nice duck," he said to Kate.

"Yup," she said, not looking up.

"A friend of yours?"

"Yup."

Kate fed Wacka a piece of bread.

"I was going to go exploring south of our camp," said John. "Your dad said there are some old caves and stuff along the bluffs. You want to come?"

"Nah," said Kate. "Wacka and I were going to spend some time at the lake."

"Huh," replied John. "Can I come?"

Kate shrugged.

"I want to go to the caves! That'd be awesome!" said Bobby. "Mum, can I go?"

"Sure," said Lisa.

"Cool! Let's go!" he said.

"All right," said John, still watching Kate. "I guess I'll see you later."

"I guess," she said.

Kate ignored the boys as they left. She pulled a long blade of grass from the ground and teased Wacka with it.

"You were a little cold, don't you think?" said her grandmother quietly as the others continued their conversation around them.

"Mmm," said Kate, not looking terribly concerned. "Maybe."

Kate didn't feel great about being rude to John, but she didn't feel like making an effort to be friendly, either. If he was only interested in chatting with her now that Aunt Bea was otherwise occupied, she didn't feel obliged to be charming in return.

CHAPTER TWENTY-TWO

BEA RAISED AN AXE ABOVE HER HEAD AND BROUGHT it down with one fluid motion. A length of wood split in two pieces with a crack and fell to the ground.

"You still haven't said when you're heading back to Ontario," said Marge. She picked up the pieces and set them on the growing pile of firewood beside them.

"Not sure," said Bea, setting another piece of wood on the block. "I kind of like the idea of spending the rest of the summer here. Maybe I'll stick around a while."

She split the wood with a single chop.

"Because of us or because of Marcus?" asked Marge.

"Mum, he's nice," said Bea. "I wish you would give this a rest."

"I just don't understand what they're doing here. I think you should keep your distance."

"Mum, I'm a grown-up."

Bea leaned the axe against the block and walked away. She pulled a handkerchief from her pocket and wiped the sweat from her face.

Kate lay face-down in the water, peering through the murk to the muddy lake bottom. Clumps of grass swayed in the current. In the shallow sections, the tips grew to within a few inches of the surface. Kate tried to imagine plunging further into the water to grab bits of grass with her teeth.

She raised her head to take a fresh breath of air and found herself staring into the face of Wacka. "Hey there," she said, treading water.

Wacka tipped her bill into the water, letting her bottom dangle in the air. She came back up and shook the water from her face before dabbling again below the surface.

Kate drifted on her back with her eyes closed. She loved the feeling of the sun on her face while the rest of her body was immersed in water. Her ears heard nothing but the low rumble of the water around her.

She opened her eyes to watch clouds pass overhead. One looked like a horse's head. Another looked like Newfoundland. Or was it Cape Breton? Just as she was trying to decide, something emerged from the water next to her. Kate gasped.

"*Wacka*," quacked the duck as she climbed onto Kate's body and made herself at home on her chest.

"I'm not a boat!" laughed Kate. She let the duck hitch a ride for a few moments before tossing her playfully into the water. Wacka made a big production of flapping and quacking, but she was clearly having a good time. Kate smiled and wished that humans were as easy to get along with as ducks.

She rolled over and swam with slow strokes toward the shore. Sometime in the last few minutes, her aunt had arrived at the lakeside.

"Oh, hi," said Kate.

"Hey," said Bea, forcing a smile.

"What's wrong?" asked Kate, stepping out of the water.

"Nothing," replied Bea. "Just parent stuff, y'know?"

"Tell me about it," said Kate, rolling her eyes. Bea handed her a towel.

"Some other time, maybe," said Bea. "Hey, you want to do something with me tonight?"

"Sure, what?" asked Kate.

"Marcus wants to go bowling."

"Okay," said Kate suspiciously. "Just the three of us?"

"Yes," said Bea. "The three of us, and John."

"Oh," said Kate. She swallowed hard.

"Is that a problem?" asked Bea.

In the weeks since the full moon, Kate hadn't spoken more than a few words to John. Frosty relations can be habit-forming; she was getting used to ignoring his attempts to make friends. As the days passed, his attempts had become fewer. She didn't really want to spend time with him, but just now she couldn't think of a good reason not to.

"No," said Kate finally. "I guess not."

"Good," said Bea, getting up and dusting herself off. "Be ready for 7:30."

CHAPTER TWENTY-THREE

KATE SAT IN SILENCE ON A COLD PLASTIC BENCH beside John. The sounds of laughter and chatter around them was interrupted every few seconds by the hollow crash of a bowling ball knocking into a set of wooden pins.

"There's a cheery couple," said Bea approaching from the front desk. She handed John and Kate their rented bowling shoes. "Marcus and I are going to go over to the snack counter. You guys want anything?"

"No thanks," said Kate. She unlaced a pair of old brown and black leather shoes as Bea and Marcus walked off.

John kicked off his sneakers and picked up one of his bowling shoes. "You ever stop to wonder how many people have worn these?" he asked, holding it up. "I bet hundreds, if not thousands."

Kate said nothing. John sighed and pushed on.

"Have I ever told you my theory about bowling?" he asked. He waited a moment for the response he knew wasn't coming. "It's pretty complex. You ready? *People hate bowling.*"

"That's it?" said Kate flatly. "'People hate bowling'?"

"Yup," said John. "Pretty fabulous, eh?"

"Genius," she said, tying her shoes.

"Look around," said John. "See the evidence. Why do most people come bowling? Because they have nothing better to do, and they forget how much they hated bowling the last time they went."

"Okay," said Kate. "What about those people?"

She pointed at a family bowling two lanes over. They were laughing. They were smiling. A teenaged girl threw a strike to the great applause of her family.

"Poor slobs," said Kate. "They look miserable."

"Ah, but they're obviously playing their first game. The first game always goes great," said John. "Look at the people in the next lane. They're showing classic second-game symptoms."

He was right. This party was decidedly less enthusiastic. The father sat at the desk, scowling in deep concentration at the score sheet.

"See? No one bowls as good in their second game as they did in their first. They're a little bummed out, a little cranky. At least one person starts to get obsessed with the score, and another person tries to keep it fun by being silly."

As John finished his sentence, a boy attempted to roll the ball backwards through his legs.

Kate smiled. "What about those people?" she said, motioning to a family at the end of the alley.

"Game three," said John. He shook his head. "Everyone is tired. The night has dragged on longer than they expected. Most of the group wants to go home, but the person obsessed with the score keeps saying that they '*paid* for three games, so they're going to *play* three games.'"

The kids in this group sat slumped on their seats. A girl about Kate's age had already changed back into her street shoes and looked ready to leave.

"People hate bowling," repeated John as Bea and Marcus arrived with an armful of snacks.

"Okay!" said Bea with great enthusiasm. "So, we've paid for three games! Let's *do* this!"

Marcus grabbed the score sheet, studying it intently. He held the tip of the tiny pencil to his lips.

Kate put her hand to her mouth to stifle a laugh. Her cheeks turned bright red.

"What?" asked Marcus. "What's so funny?"

"Nothing," said John with a grin. He looked at Kate. "We're just really excited about bowling."

CHAPTER TWENTY-FOUR

"BUT WE PAID FOR THREE GAMES," MARCUS WAS arguing two hours later.

"Okay, Dad. We got it," said John. "We just want to go, all right? You guys enjoy the rest of your night."

"Oh, let them go," said Bea. "They're tired."

"Well," said Marcus, looking from Bea to John. "Okay."

John yanked off his shoes and wiggled his toes. "Sweet freedom," he said.

"I just need to stop at the bathroom before we go," said Kate.

"I'll join you," said Bea. She grabbed Kate's arm and pulled her toward the bathrooms.

Marcus sat across from his son and watched him lace up his sneakers. "You like this girl," said Marcus.

John shrugged.

"Yeah, well, we're not going to be around here forever," said Marcus.

"I like it here."

"It's only a matter of time. You know that."

John sat still for a minute. "When?" he asked finally.

"I don't know," said Marcus. "Soon."

"What about Bea?" said John.

"What about her?" said Marcus.

John stared at his dad a moment. "It just seems, like, maybe you like her," he said. "And maybe that's enough reason to stick around."

Marcus sighed. "We've been over this a million times. We can't *stay* anywhere. Ever."

"But I don't get…" began John.

"No. No, you don't," said Marcus as Bea and Kate approached from across the bowling alley. He lowered his voice. "And maybe it's time you were grown up enough to start getting it."

"Such serious faces," said Bea as she arrived, looking back and forth between Marcus and John. "What are you guys talking about?"

"Nothing," said John. He turned to Kate. "You ready?"

She nodded. "Let's go."

Bea sat next to Marcus on the bench. She leaned into him as they watched Kate and John walk out the front door and into the night.

"They're sweet," said Bea.

"Yeah," said Marcus. He wrapped an arm around her shoulders. His mouth smiled but his eyes didn't.

CHAPTER TWENTY-FIVE

"IT'S SO DARK," SAID KATE. SHE COULD JUST barely see John walking beside her on the gravel road. Had Kate not walked this way hundreds of times, it would have been nearly impossible to find where they were going.

"No moon," pointed out John. "It won't rise for another hour. It'll be full in a few nights," he said. He thought a few moments as they slowly walked on. "We never talked about last month. What happened?"

Kate shrugged. "I don't know. I just felt like quacking and..." she mimed flapping her wings.

"But how did you know to do that?"

"I just knew, I guess," she said. "I knew I wasn't a wolf. I don't know how any of this works, but I just never felt like one."

Their feet crunched softly in the gravel as they walked.

"I've been wondering about that," said John, "what I would do if I had the chance to do it again for the first time."

He looked up as he walked, searching the empty sky.

"What would you do?" asked Kate.

"I think I'd howl," he said. "I always knew I was a wolf, even when I was a little kid."

"That's cool," said Kate, nodding. "Cool that you knew."

"Yeah," he said.

They walked quietly.

"It's so dark," repeated Kate.

She felt John's hand touch the back of hers. His index finger hooked around her pinky. They walked with their fingers locked for a few strides before she slid her hand into his.

They walked holding hands, chatting easily. Kate didn't pause to wonder whether this was the right thing to do. Like becoming a duck, it just felt right. She didn't want anything to stop this.

"Hold on a sec," said John. His pace slowed down as Kate's heart sped up. He stopped and turned to face her.

"What?" asked Kate softly.

"It's just…" he put his hand on her shoulder.

Kate shut her eyes.

"Is there a light on in that house over there?" he asked.

"What," said Kate blankly.

"Look," said John, turning her around and pointing into the dark. "That house. I think it's the old one with the broken windows and stuff. It looks like there's a light on in the upstairs window."

"That's stupid," said Kate. "No one lives there. Why would there be...."

Her words trailed off as she noticed a dim light, like that of a candle, flickering from an upper window of the house.

"Let's check it out," said John, already walking towards the house.

"But," stammered Kate, "I thought we were..." She kicked at the gravel. "Busy."

"C'mon!" called John, striding away.

"*But*..." whispered Kate. She gritted her teeth. "I'm coming!"

CHAPTER TWENTY-SIX

DIRK SAT AT HIS TYPEWRITER. HE'D BEEN STARING at blank piece of paper for the better part of the last fifteen minutes.

"Think, Bragg," he said to himself. "Think, think, think...."

He had been prolific these last few weeks. This house had been good to him. The morning after moving in, he'd stocked the pantry with the food he'd need for the month—mostly bananas, dried fruit, and jars of sauerkraut. The only evidence from the outside that anyone had been living in the house was the occasional *tap-tap-tapping* sound from an upstairs window. Dirk had set up his old manual typewriter in one of the bedrooms, writing story after story for *Really Real News* and sending them by mail to his editor in New York.

Sandra was very happy. Dirk used the *Really Real News*'s unofficial motto as his guide to writing: *If you can't report the truth, just make sure it's interesting.*

He'd written stories about panda bears opening a trendy vegetarian restaurant in New Jersey ("Today's Special: Bamboo"), Elvis coming out of hiding to take a run at the United States presidency, and about how the union representing garbage men in New York City was plotting to overthrow the mayor. Tonight, he was drawing a blank.

"Think, think, think..." repeated Dirk. "How about a story...about..." he stood up and paced the room, "...cats? *Here kitty, kitty, kitty.* Kitty-cat. Kitty Litter. Kitty..." he scrunched his forehead as searched for a word, "Zombies? Kitty zombies? *Adorable Zombie Cats Take Over The Internet.* BRILLIANT!"

He jumped back into his seat, put a pencil between his teeth, and placed his hands on the typewriter keys.

He paused. He heard a sound.

Dirk sat with his fingers suspended above the typewriter.

He heard footsteps and muted voices downstairs.

Someone was in the house.

CHAPTER TWENTY-SEVEN

"THIS IS STUPID," WHISPERED KATE AS SHE WALKED behind John through the front door. "Stupid and dangerous. We don't know who is in here."

"You never want to have any fun," answered John.

"Your idea of fun usually involves breaking and entering," she hissed back.

They stood in the kitchen and tried to let their eyes adjust to the darkness. They could see very little.

"What is that smell?" asked John.

"Stinks like overripe bananas," said Kate. She sniffed again, "And something sour. What's that rotten cabbage stuff called?"

"Sauerkraut," said John, scrunching his nose. He stepped into a room with an old couch.

"Seriously," said Kate. "Let's go. I don't need to know who is camping in this house. I don't even want to know. This place is creepy."

"What if it's someone looking for werewolves?"

"Why would they be here?" said Kate.

"Um, duh," said John, pointing back and forth between them. "Two werewolf families living next door to each other? Dirt Bag already almost found us. Why not someone else?"

Kate peered around the shadowy room. "Do you think it's Dirt Bag?"

"Dunno," said John.

"What if it's someone who just wants to be left alone?"

"Then we'll apologize and leave them alone," said John. "And maybe offer to buy them a case of rotten cabbage."

At the far end of the room, a doorway opened on a flight of stairs leading up.

"Ladies first," whispered John.

"No, no," said Kate. "I insist. Guys with stupid ideas first."

They crept to the top of the dark stairs. Two doors led off the landing. One led to a bathroom. The other was closed.

"That's the room that faces the road," whispered Kate. "That's where the light was coming from."

"What should we do, just knock?" said John.

"This is so stupid," said Kate. "Let's just go."

John rapped lightly on the door. The sound echoed through the old house.

"No reply," said John.

"Um, duh," whispered Kate.

They waited in silence outside of the room.

"Now what?" asked Kate.

"A little something I like to call 'opening the door…'" said John.

He reached for the doorknob, turned, and pushed.

A faint smell of smoke drifted from the room as the door opened.

"Someone just snuffed a candle," said Kate "Smell it?"

John nodded and walked into the room. "So where's the candle? And where is the person who snuffed it?"

But for a wooden crate by the window, the room was empty.

CHAPTER TWENTY-EIGHT

DIRK COULDN'T BELIEVE HIS LUCK.

He fiddled with the settings on his camera as the sound of a woman singing country music—badly—drifted across the bar.

It had been a narrow escape. All the practicing he had done in the last few weeks—throwing all his worldly possessions into his bag, stuffing the bulky typewriter into a pillowcase, and escaping through the bedroom window—had paid off when it mattered. By the time those bickering kids made it to the upstairs landing, he was already halfway to his truck.

He took a sip of his beer and leaned back in his chair. It was good to be back in civilization, such as it was. He'd slept the rest of the night in the back of his truck, which he'd hidden on an old logging road several hundred meters into the woods behind the abandoned house. He'd then woken early and driven far enough away that he was sure he wouldn't accidentally run into any of the werewolf family. He'd checked into a dirty motel a few towns away from the werewolf camp, called Sandra, then made his way to this seedy country-and-western bar to celebrate his good fortune.

The wolf story was locked up. In two days, the moon would be full. He'd sneak back to nab the pictures, video, and story that would land him on the front page of every newspaper in the country.

Even better, his editor just told him she'd booked him on the national TV show *America This Morning*. As soon as he had his proof, he would drive to the closest TV studio and expose the story to the world.

But, of all the luck, who would have believed this backwoods town in the middle of New Brunswick had a karaoke bar? Dirk looked around the room to the small, mid-afternoon crowd assembled.

They are about to get the show of their lives, he thought.

The bartender tapped him on the shoulder to indicate it was his turn. Dirk set his camera on the table, pointed it at the stage, and hit the *record* button.

He ran his hand through his greasy hair as he climbed the stairs to the stage and stepped up to the microphone. That familiar wave of nervous excitement washed over him as the first few notes of steel guitar echoed around the tiny bar. He pulled the microphone to his mouth and began to sing.

Baby, I'm a drivin' fer yer looove.
But baby, I hope yer not abooove
waitin' fer me, and the love that I proviiide'
'cause baby, I can't live without this ride.

The music swelled as it climbed toward the chorus. Dirk threw his arm in the air and sang passionately into the microphone.

"My wheels belong to the road, but my heart—belongs to yooooou!"

The half-dozen people in the bar cheered. They rose to their feet as he belted out the final chorus of the song.

Dirk gave a modest bow, waving away the applause. He returned to his table and switched off the recorder on his camera. Dirk usually recorded his karaoke sessions so he could critique his performance later on in private. He was pretty sure this one would make it to his highlight reel.

CHAPTER TWENTY-NINE

"MAYBE IT'S HAUNTED," SUGGESTED BOBBY, AS HE looked around the empty room.

In the light of the morning, the house didn't seem so scary to Kate. It just seemed dirty, old, and empty.

"Ghosts don't eat sauerkraut," said Kate. "From the looks of the mess downstairs, someone's been living here a while."

"I don't get how you could see the light in the window and find the whole place empty," said Bobby. "It just doesn't make sense. You said you could smell the candle, right?"

"Right," said John.

Kate looked at John's face. He was so serious. He'd given no indication this morning that anything had happened between them the night before. She was beginning to feel as if she'd imagined it. She placed her hand on his back.

"What is it?" she asked.

He stepped away from her touch and approached the window.

"It's a long way down," he said. He ran his fingers along the window sash, grabbed hold, and pulled. Despite its age, the window opened easily. He peeked his head out the window and looked down. "Well, would you look at that."

"What?" asked Kate.

"Come on," said John, as he swung his leg over the window sill and climbed out. A narrow balcony, invisible from the road, ran along the edge of the roof just below the window.

"A widow's walk," said John.

"What's a widow's walk?" asked Bobby, following him onto the ledge.

"You see them a lot in old fishing towns," explained John. "We saw a bunch of them in Maine and Boston when we lived down there," his eyes fixed on the horizon. "You can see a long way from here. On a clear day, you could probably see the Bay of Fundy."

"But what's it for?" asked Kate.

"A fishermen's wife would come out here after a storm to watch the fishing boats come in," said John. "The longer she waited for her husband's boat to come home, the more likely the boat was lost at sea. She'd pace up and down this walkway until she knew he wasn't coming back."

Kate shuddered. "That's so sad."

John nodded. He looked down. "See? It wouldn't have been that hard for someone to climb down. It's not that far of a drop from that ledge to the ground."

"Okay," said Kate sitting with her legs dangling over the ledge. "So we know how they got away, but we still don't know who it was."

"I bet it was Dirt Bag," said John.

"I thought he gave up on finding wolves here."

"Whoever it was really didn't want us to find them," said John.

"That doesn't' mean it's Dirt Bag."

"No, but it kind of seems like him," said John. He shielded his eyes from the sun and stared off toward the bay.

"You going to tell your dad?" asked Bobby.

"No," he answered shortly.

"Why not?" asked Kate.

John paused.

"He'd just get paranoid and say we have to leave. We always have to leave just when I'm starting to like it somewhere."

Kate flushed. "So, what are we going to do?" she asked.

"Something," he said. "The full moon is in two days. And if it *is* Dirt Bag, he's here for us."

CHAPTER THIRTY

KATE'S BARE FEET DRIPPED WITH DEW AS SHE walked through the grass toward the lake. The morning sun was just starting to dissolve the thin layer of fog resting on the water. The lonely call of a passing loon drifted from overhead.

Kate came to the lake to be alone, but as she approached, she could see someone sitting on the shore. It was Bea. She sat hugging her knees and watching the water. As Kate got closer, she could see her eyes were red and puffy.

"Hey, are you okay?" asked Kate. She sat beside her.

"Fine," said Bea. She sniffed and forced a smile. "Fine if you like heartbreak, which I seem to be a glutton for."

"Oh, Aunt Bea," said Kate. "What happened?"

Bea closed her eyes. "You ever notice the harder you try to take things nice and easy the more likely they end up being stupid and hard?"

Kate's lip quivered.

"Of course you know," said Bea, recognizing some of her own feelings on her niece's face. She wrapped her arm around Kate. Kate leaned against her for support and sniffed back her own tears.

"Look at us," said Bea, laughing in spite of herself. "We're pathetic."

"I thought the pathetic thing went away when you grew up."

"I wish," said Bea. "So what about you? Is it John?"

Kate nodded. "I don't even want to like him, but I can't help it. And the other night...I was sure he felt the same way I do, it was amazing."

"Amazing," repeated Bea.

"But now it's like nothing happened. I feel stupid and small, like he thinks I'm just one of his little buddies, like Bobby." She wiped her eyes on the sleeve of her sweater. "What about you?"

"Same old story," said Bea. "Girl meets boy. Girl falls for boy. Boy tells girl he's moving away. Boy invites girl to come with him...."

"What?"

"Yeah. And boy tells girl she shouldn't ever expect to see her family again."

"You're joking."

Bea shook her head. She looked into Kate's eyes. "He says he and John never go back to the same spot twice. They never look back. They just keep going."

"You aren't going to go with them, are you?"

"No," said Bea. "It's really nice with him. I was almost ready to say I love him. But I can't do that."

"Good," said Kate. "When are they leaving?"

"Tomorrow morning. After the full moon."

Kate picked up a stone and flicked it into the water.

"So at least both of our problems will be gone by this time tomorrow," she said.

CHAPTER THIRTY-ONE

MARGE STOOD IN FRONT OF THE CABIN WITH HER arms crossed.

"Repeat after me," she said. "I promise...."

"Grandma, this is stupid," said Bobby. "I'll stay put. I swear."

"I said, *repeat after me*," said Marge. "I promise...."

Bobby sighed. "I promise..." he repeated.

"...that I will stay in this cabin all night," said Marge.

"...that I will stay in this cabin all night."

"No matter what," she said.

"No matter what."

"And if I leave...."

"And if I leave..." he repeated.

"I'll do the dishes for a month and be in charge of hauling firewood for the rest of my natural life."

Bobby paused. "The rest of my life?"

"*Say it.*"

"Okay, okay," he said. "Dishes for a month and firewood for the rest of my life. Happy now?"

"Ecstatic," said his grandmother. She kissed his forehead. "Good night. Sweet dreams."

"Thanks, Grandma," said Bobby.

He retreated to the cabin and shut the door. He watched through the window as his grandma and parents chatted and tended to the campfire. After a few minutes, they hiked toward the woods and disappeared into the foliage.

Bobby paced up and down in the cabin. "I hope John and Kate know what they're doing," he said to himself.

He glanced out the window one last time before slipping out of the cabin and into the woods. "This better be worth a lifetime of hauling firewood."

CHAPTER THIRTY-TWO

MARCUS STOOD ALONE IN THE CLEARING, watching the sky as it changed from blue to pink. Suddenly he heard a rustling in the brush nearby.

"Is that you?" he called.

Dirk emerged from the shadows. "Sorry, I got a bit turned around in the woods." He absently fiddled with the settings on his camera. His eyes flared with giddy excitement. "Oh, man. This is going to be great."

"They'll be here any minute," said Marcus.

"All right," said Dirk, glancing around the space to make sure they were alone. "Just point me at a spot where I can hide with my camera, and I'm out of your hair."

Marcus took a deep breath. "Listen," he said. "Maybe I'm having second thoughts about this."

"You can't have second thoughts," said Dirk, becoming serious. "I've been working on this story for years. I've been living in a mouldy old house for the last month."

"I'll pay you," said Marcus.

Dirk scoffed. "I don't want money. A deal is a deal: you deliver me werewolves, and I'll never bother you again," he paused. "Look, don't worry. After tonight, I've never heard of you. You're free."

Marcus let out a long sigh and looked back at the sky. "It's just...."

"Just *nothing*," said Dirk. "We had a deal. You contacted *me*, remember?"

Marcus pursed his lips. "All right," he said. He pointed across the clearing. "You see that maple? There's an easy spot to climb to that's concealed from the clearing. You'll have a full view of everything."

The sound of distant voices drifted up the trail.

"Better hurry," said Marcus.

Dirk scurried into the trees.

Marcus nodded to himself as he made a silent decision. He was sick of running. Sick of slinking away at the slightest sign of danger. Sick of dragging his son from place to place. Sick of never being able to find new friends, let alone new love. He'd been running for nearly fifteen years—since the fire that took everything from him. His wife. His freedom. His life.

Maybe John was right. Maybe Bea was worth staying for. He could see now there was just one obstacle standing in his way.

Dirk Bragg wasn't going to make it out of the woods tonight alive.

CHAPTER THIRTY-THREE

KATE'S FEET CRUNCHED ON THE GRAVEL OF THE trail as she tried to keep pace with John.

"Why don't you just tell your dad?" she said for the third time. "If you guys are leaving tomorrow anyway, what's the difference?"

John maintained his stride and stared straight ahead. "Because *we* have a plan, that's why."

"But maybe he can help us. Maybe we can tell my parents, too," argued Kate.

"We don't need their help," said John. "As long as Bobby does his job, we'll be fine."

"I don't like this," said Kate.

"You think I do?" said John. He stopped. "I don't want to leave tomorrow. I feel like if we can do this ourselves, maybe I don't have to leave."

"But your dad said—"

"I don't care what he said," interrupted John. He looked at the ground.

"Did you guys have a fight?"

"Another fight, you mean."

Kate touched his arm.

"I think the sun's about to set," said John. "We should go."

A few minutes later, they entered the clearing to find Marcus standing by himself in the moonlight.

"I was beginning to think no one was coming," he said.

John and Kate said nothing.

"Still not talking to me, huh?" said Marcus. "*Great.* Did you at least finish packing?"

John dug his hands into his pockets and stared at his dad.

"*Did you finish packing?*" repeated Marcus.

"Yes," said John.

"Good."

Bea stepped into the clearing from the trail. She stopped abruptly when she saw Marcus.

"I suppose you're not speaking to me either," said Marcus.

Bea slowly exhaled before answering. "What would you like me to say?"

Before Marcus could answer, Kate's parents and grandmother entered the clearing.

"Sorry we're late," said Brian, rubbing his hands together and looking at the sky. He was clearly oblivious to the tension in the group. "Sun's about to set. Everyone ready?"

"Ready," said Marcus.

"Your second night as a duck," said Lisa to Kate. "Big plans for the evening?"

Kate looked at John. "We've a few things we want to do, yeah," said Kate.

The group turned to the west. The only sound was the light breeze in the leaves overhead. They watched as the sun slipped below the horizon.

"*Whooooo?*" came the call. "*Whooooo?*"

CHAPTER THIRTY-FOUR

DIRK WAS DUMBFOUNDED.

He had been prepared for some amazing sights, but what unfolded through his viewfinder was stranger than he'd ever imagined.

At first, most everything happened just as he had expected. As the sun set, the group turned toward the moon. Most of the group called out in a collective howl and transformed into a pack of wolves. But the girl... he couldn't believe it.

The girl *quacked*. Like a *duck*.

Each subsequent quack from her mouth sounded less human and more...duck-like. Dirk trained his camera on the girl and recorded video as she transformed before his eyes into a small brown duck. He followed her flight with his camera as she left the clearing.

Dirk was so distracted by the duck that he lost track of which person became which wolf—except for Marcus.

The giant black wolf was difficult to miss. A spiked ridge of fur at his shoulder blades made him appear even bigger and more intimidating. He sat silently in the middle of the clearing as the rest of the wolves dispersed into the forest.

Dirk stayed perched in his tree, watching. He would wait until Marcus left, then sneak into the forest to grab a few more candid photos before he hit the road. He had an early morning date with a TV studio and international acclaim.

The big black wolf sat holding its lonely vigil with the moon. Ten minutes passed, then twenty. Dirk's leg fell asleep. He adjusted his weight in the tree.

The noise from the branches stirred Marcus from his trance. He turned to face Dirk's tree.

"Nice doggy," said Dirk, causally pulling a banana from his jacket pocket and peeling it open. "Want a treat?" A low growl erupted from deep within the black giant. Dirk felt the blood drain from his hands and face. The grin faded from his lips. The banana peel fell to the ground.

Marcus padded slowly to the base of the tree. His growl deepened. His eyes shot an unmistakable look of hatred at the dishevelled man in the tree.

A lump rose in Dirk's throat. He now understood what a mistake it had been to make a deal with a werewolf.

CHAPTER THIRTY-FIVE

BOBBY THOUGHT ABOUT HOW SIMPLE THEIR PLAN had been, and how it had already gone so wrong.

His job had been to watch the clearing for any sign of Dirt Bag. That's how he'd come to be lying flat on his stomach beneath a bush at the edge of the clearing. Once he found Dirt Bag, he was to sneak off to find John.

If Dirt Bag *was* in the woods, as they suspected, he'd need his truck to get away. Kate's assignment was to survey the forest from above, find the truck, and lead John and Bobby to it.

Once Dirt Bag showed up at his truck at the end of the evening, they'd have a little chat. Bobby would explain that if Dirt Bag didn't hand over his evidence—likely his camera's memory card—Bobby would sick his "wolf-friend" on him. At this point in the conversation, John would growl and try to look as wild and menacing as possible. They were pretty sure Dirt Bag would see things their way.

Their simple plan didn't account for what Bobby was watching unfold in the clearing.

"Hey, Marcus," called Dirk from his tree. "Can't we talk about this? I mean, we had a deal, right?"

Marcus growled again.

"Right," said Dirk. "Listen, *heh*, *heh*, maybe we're having difficulty with our inter-species communication. See, I've never spoken with a werewolf before. Maybe you *aren't* threatening me like it seems you are. So... give two howls if you really want to, y'know, kill me, or three quick yips if you don't."

Marcus's growl was immediate and deep.

Dirk yelped and scrambled higher in his tree. His sweaty palms clung desperately to the bark.

"Remember that chat we had just a few minutes ago? That one about me just forgetting this werewolf story? I think it's a great idea. In fact, *what* werewolves? Am I *right?*"

Bobby glanced back and forth between the reporter and the giant wolf. This was *bad*. He needed to find John and Kate before it was too late. They hated the idea of Dirt Bag writing about them in his paper, but they didn't want him dead.

Bobby crawled slowly along the ground away from the clearing. Once he was far enough away, he rose to his feet and crept silently through the forest.

CHAPTER THIRTY-SIX

MARCUS APPROACHED A PATCH OF UNDERBRUSH at the edge of the clearing. He was sure he'd heard something.

It took just a few sniffs of the ground for Marcus to know who had been there—little boys have distinctive smells. Bobby had been watching. So he knew Dirt Bag was there. And he knew Marcus had invited him. If the boy told anyone, it would ruin everything.

Marcus and John had moved so many times trying to evade the reporter. There had been many close calls. It took years for Marcus to realize he could use Dirk: make him an ally. All he had to do was promise to give the reporter the very thing he'd been searching for: evidence of werewolves.

It isn't easy finding other werewolves. He'd chased down so many rumours that had turned out to be nothing—in each case either the pack had long since left, or it never existed in the first place.

Marcus discovered these Canadian wolves a few months earlier. He had chased one of those rumours—an article in the local weekly newspaper about a man who swore he'd heard the howling of wolves. The paper quoted local wildlife officials who said it was impossible: wolves had been eradicated from this part of the country for more than a hundred years.

Still, Marcus thought it was worth a check.

John was never much of a bother when Marcus was searching. He slept through most full moons. Marcus walked all night in a grid pattern as if he were searching for a lost child. So many times, his search turned up nothing. This time, he found what he was after. Wolves. And a story for Dirt Bag.

Marcus contacted him soon after. He confessed to be the wolf that Bragg had pursued over several years through several states. He made the deal over the phone. He would deliver Bragg a pack of unsuspecting wolves. All Marcus asked for in return was to be left alone.

But the deal was off. The reporter had to die. And now that Bobby knew what was going on, well, he had to die, too.

Marcus stitched a new plan together in his head. He was sure no one would miss Dirt Bag. Bobby was a bit trickier.

His parents couldn't go to the police. Only a handful of people in the nearby town had a vague idea that anyone even lived out here. Bea had told him that, officially, none of the members of that family even existed. They'd have a hard time explaining to the police that a boy with no birth certificate, no health records, and no school registration had gone missing.

There would be no reason to suspect foul play or Marcus. The family would just have to come to accept that Bobby was gone. Little boys sometimes run away. And since Bea would be shattered by the news of her missing nephew, maybe Marcus could help her pick up the pieces.

Marcus looked to the tree where Dirt Bag sat trembling in fear. He wasn't going anywhere. Surely, Marcus had time to track down the brat, take care of him, and still finish off the reporter before sunrise.

He plunged into the woods. The boy had a few minutes' lead on him, but Marcus could make up the distance.

Minutes later, he heard Bobby's clumsy human footsteps ahead of him in the forest. But he could hear something else.

Another wolf.

Marcus stopped and slunk low to the ground. He couldn't take down the boy in front of one of the others. He would wait for his chance. There were still a few hours of darkness left.

Perched in his tree, Dirk assessed the situation. This was the worst predicament he'd ever been in—even worse than that time he was tied up in that Vegas dressing room while working on a story about an artsy troupe of Martian circus performers. Marcus wanted to kill him.

But Dirk had a more immediate problem. He had to pee. Really badly.

Where Marcus had gone, and why he had left so quickly, Dirk could not guess. But with the big wolf gone, he decided it was time to take care of business. He scrambled to the ground and found an appropriate bush.

Dirk considered his options. Only he knew where he had hidden his truck. He had no idea how soon Marcus would return to finish him off, but the desire to get away from this place and plop himself in front of a television camera was strong.

Dirk ran into the woods. In spite of the still very real danger, he smiled. In five minutes he would be speeding his way toward fame, and with any hope, a proper breakfast.

CHAPTER THIRTY-SEVEN

"MARCUS WANTS TO KILL DIRT BAG!" SAID BOBBY.

Two blank faces stared back at him. The duck and the wolf didn't seem to have trouble believing he'd found Dirk. What was harder to swallow was the idea that John's dad was about to murder him.

John shook his head. He knew his dad was an angry man. He knew his anger had recently grown into a brooding darkness that never seemed to go away. He knew how much Marcus hated Dirt Bag. He just couldn't believe his dad was a killer.

Without waiting for further explanation, John sprinted through brush and trees toward the clearing with Bobby and Kate following close behind. They arrived to find it empty.

No Dirt Bag. No Marcus.

"I swear, they were right here," said Bobby. He scrambled up Dirk's tree. "Maybe Dirt Bag left a mark, or dropped something, or...."

John approached the base of the tree. He had no idea why Bobby would be lying about his dad, but that was the only explanation. He sat on the ground and took a deep breath of night air.

He smelled something.

He inhaled again, his heightened canine sense of smell identifying the different aromas of the forest. Trees, grass, moss, earth. And something else.

He followed the scent to the other side of tree and found its source on a bush: human urine.

There were other smells: unwashed clothes. Sauerkraut. John followed the trail of scents and came across the discarded peel of a banana. He picked it up.

"What?" asked Bobby.

John turned back to Bobby and Kate. The yellow peel dangled from his mouth.

"Banana," whispered Bobby. "It's Dirt Bag, right?"

John dropped the peel and took a few more steps into the woods. He smelled something else, something familiar.

"Marcus is following him," said Bobby. He jumped to the ground.

John nodded.

"I told you. He's going to kill him," said Bobby. "We've got to stop him."

John paused, then nodded again.

"Let's go!" said Bobby.

"*Quack!*" said Kate. She flapped her wings and flew into the air.

CHAPTER THIRTY-EIGHT

DIRK FOUND HIS TRUCK PARKED ON A LONG-forgotten logging road hidden under a layer of branches. He breathed a sigh of relief. His camera was full of images that would prove the existence of werewolves. He had a juicy story full of sneaky deals, deception, danger, and—of all things—a wereduck.

He pulled the branches off his truck and rehearsed in his mind what he would say later that morning on national television.

I always knew in my heart that werewolves were real, but I never knew to what level of physical danger I would have to put myself through to prove it. Had I known that my very life was on the line, I may have been too terrified to attempt it, but in the end, I believe the truth is worth it.

He chuckled. People would eat it up.

He removed the last branch from the hood and reached for the door handle. As his fingers touched the steel, a low growl rumbled directly behind him.

Dirk turned slowly around, hoping to find any other creature in the world but Marcus.

The giant black wolf stood just paces away, his body slung low, ready to pounce.

"Oh! *There* you are," said Dirk with a nervous squeak, pressing his back against the truck. Marcus's teeth dripped saliva into the dust.

"Yeah, like, I was hoping we might talk again about that deal...."

Dirk snuck his hand behind his body and grasped the door handle. "Y'know—the one where I don't write about you or your son, and I, um, live?"

Dirk pulled up on the handle. It was locked.

"*Oh, crap,*" he whimpered.

Dirk prayed for a miracle. It came from the sky.

A meteor of brown feathers crashed with a *boomph!* into the roof of Dirk's truck and began to scream quacks at them.

The duck distracted Marcus just long enough for Dirk to slip his hand inside his pants pocket. He found the cold metal and plastic of his car keys and pressed the *unlock* button on the remote.

Ca-chunk!

The mechanical sound pulled Marcus's attention back to Dirk. He growled. Marcus wouldn't hesitate again. Dirk shut his eyes and braced for Dirk's attack.

"*Oh, crap,*" he whimpered again.

Before Marcus could act, he was distracted again: this time by the roaring charge of another beast emerging from the woods.

Dirk dared a peek through one eye and saw a second, smaller wolf locked in combat with Marcus.

Marcus was surprised by his attacker, but he quickly regained the advantage. Snarling and growling, he flipped the smaller wolf onto its back, pinning it to the ground, his jaws clamped around its neck. The duck hopped to the ground, quacking desperately.

Fascinating as the whole scene was, Dirk didn't feel like sticking around to see how it would end. He jumped into his truck and turned the key in the ignition. The truck's tires spun briefly in the dirt before skidding away.

The duck flapped its wings at Marcus, pecking at his hind legs. Annoyed, Marcus released his attacker and lunged at the duck. His teeth sunk into its flesh. He gave the duck one mighty shake and dropped its limp body to the ground.

CHAPTER THIRTY-NINE

JOHN EMERGED FROM THE WOODS WITH BOBBY and Kate close behind. He surveyed the scene and saw what his father had done. On the ground beside Marcus lay the lifeless body of a duck. An injured black wolf was just picking itself up from the ground.

"Grandma!" yelled Bobby. "And Wacka?"

Rage welled up within John. In that moment, without taking time to dwell upon the consequences, his allegiance became clear.

John charged, growling and gnashing, toward his father, knocking him into the dirt. Marcus lay stunned, looking into the snarling face of his son. He rose up and bared his teeth.

John stood tall. He was joined this time by Marge, who was ready again to fight. Bobby was there, too. And Kate.

"You need to go now, Marcus," said Bobby. The group advanced. "You need to go far away and never bother us again."

Marcus stood his ground. He growled.

Kate couldn't stop herself. She threw herself at the giant wolf. She hated him for what he'd done to her grandmother and to Wacka. She flapped. She quacked. She scratched and pecked, forcing him to continue his slow retreat.

Bobby landed a kick into Marcus's haunch. The giant wolf let out a surprised yelp.

John and Marge stood shoulder to shoulder, hackles raised.

Marcus looked into the faces of his attackers. This wasn't how this night was supposed to turn out. It couldn't end now, not like this. He took one last look deep into the eyes of his son and saw only contempt.

He turned and fled into what remained of the night.

The group stood frozen for a moment. Marge was the first to move. As she laid down to lick her wounds, her grandchildren rushed to her side. The older wolf was tired and scratched, but seemed okay.

Kate waddled toward the body of Wacka. Streaks of blood stained the feathers of her breast. Kate laid her head upon her friend's wing. She was still breathing.

"*Wacka*," said the injured duck softly.

Bobby knelt at her side. "Think she'll be all right?" he asked.

Kate looked at her brother. She hoped so.

"What about you, John. You okay?" asked Bobby. He placed his hand on the wolf's head.

John stood staring down the logging road.

"Dirt Bag got away," muttered Bobby, understanding at once.

The group was silent.

"He's got pictures of us," said Bobby finally. He shook his head. "There's no way we could catch him now. Not without wings."

Bobby, John, and Marge turned as one to look at Kate.

CHAPTER FORTY

DIRK STEERED HIS TRUCK FROM A SMALL DIRT road onto the highway. He popped the shifter into fifth gear and smiled as the engine roared to catch up with his heavy foot pressing the gas pedal to the floor. Nothing could stop him from getting to that television studio. He switched on the radio and searched for a country music station.

At this rate, he'd never make it across the border in time to be on *America This Morning*. Luckily, one of the show's producers had found a little TV studio just an hour's drive away. By the magic of satellite, Dirk would become a journalistic celebrity in America, broadcasting from the middle of nowhere, Canada.

One of Dirk's favourite songs came on the radio. He turned it up.

Dirk looked at the clock. He was a few minutes ahead of schedule. He decided to stop in the next town to pick up a snack. He downshifted as he approached a stop sign.

Finding Dirk's truck was the easy part. Kate had followed the old logging road to a bigger road to a bigger road until she'd finally spotted the white pickup speeding onto the highway. Catching him now that he was driving at full speed was the hard part. She flew higher in the sky to keep a better eye on the truck and maybe pick up a bit of speed.

The truck drove faster than Kate could fly—that was a problem. But the truck had to follow the road, which turned and bended to follow the contours of the land. Kate found she could gain on Dirk if she flew in a straight line, as the crow flies. Still, she knew couldn't keep up this pace for long.

In a few hundred metres, she saw the truck would reach a stop sign. This might be her last chance. Her muscles burned from pumping her wings so fast, but she was making up some of the distance between herself and the truck as it slowed to a rolling stop. She flew lower as the truck pulled through the intersection; the tailgate was just barely out of her reach. She put on one last burst of speed, closed her eyes, and dived.

SLAM.

Had Dirk been paying attention to anything but the music on the radio, he would have heard the distinctive sound of three pounds of feathers, bill, and webbed feet slamming into the steel bed of a Ford Ranger pickup truck.

CHAPTER FORTY-ONE

KATE LAID STILL JUST BEHIND THE CAB OF THE truck. She shook out each wing and leg, finally deciding she hadn't broken anything. The sounds of a steady pounding beat and steel guitar spilled out of the truck's back window.

Dirk was singing along to the music. Clearly, he hadn't heard Kate's less than graceful landing. So far, so good. Now all she needed was to find Dirk's camera and delete the photos.

The only other item in the back of the truck was a dirty old knapsack. There was no way Dirk had had time to pack his camera in it before speeding off. Kate decided it must be in the cab with him.

Street lights passed overhead. The truck slowed again as it entered a small town. Kate hid behind the knapsack and listened.

The truck stopped. The driver's side door opened and shut. A bell tinkled. Kate peered over the edge of the truck's bed and saw Dirk had entered a twenty-four-hour convenience store.

She jumped to the narrow ledge beneath the truck's sliding back window, then pushed her bill into the gap between the panes. It open was just a few inches—not quite wide enough for her to squeeze her body through.

She ignored the stench of rotting food and body odour in the cab as she wedged the rest of her head inside the window. Pushing with her whole weight, she tried to pry apart the windows with her tiny shoulders.

Just a bit more....

She pushed harder and felt the glass panes budge.

A tiny bit more....

With a final push, her body popped through the narrow slot and tumbled onto the seat. She pulled herself up on two shaky webbed feet and looked around for the camera.

Dirk paced up and down the aisles of the store, looking for something to satisfy his ravenous, if particular, tastes. He picked up a bag of potato chips and scanned the list of ingredients.

"Ugh," he said. He threw the bag back on the pile.

"Is there a problem?" asked the clerk, watching him from behind the counter.

"No," said Dirk. Then under his breath: "Nothing the hydrogenated-potato mafia won't kill me over."

"What was that?" asked the man.

Dirk coughed. "Nothing. Just trying to find a snack."

Kate simultaneously discovered the camera and the source of the smell. A layer of black banana peels carpeted the floor of the truck. Sitting among the peels was Dirk's camera.

Kate hopped to the floor and examined the camera's control panel. She poked her bill at the *power* button. The display screen lit up as it came to life.

"You want *how* many pickled eggs?" asked the clerk.

"Six, please," said Dirk.

The clerk winced. For the nine years he'd worked in this store, a jar filled with eggs in cloudy yellow brine had sat on the counter. A piece of paper taped to its side said they sold for a quarter a piece. No one had ever asked for one before. Ever.

"They've been in there a long time, man," he said. "You sure about this?"

Dirk scoffed. "Of course I'm sure."

While Dirk had reservations about DNA tampering in chicken eggs, *everyone* knew the brain-control side effects were neutralized by pickling brine. Besides, he was pretty sure these eggs predated the government's mind-control technology.

The clerk unscrewed the lid and plunged his hand into the cold liquid. He fished out six eggs and placed them in a large paper cup.

"Is that it?" he asked, wiping his hands on a paper towel. He reached for the bottle of hand sanitizer he kept under the counter. He wanted to bathe his arm in it.

"Just these," said Dirk. He slid a bunch of bananas across the counter. "And a couple of these," he said, grabbing a few sticks of beef jerky from a box beside the cash register.

The man rang up Dirk's total and began counting change. Dirk looked at his watch. He needed to get back on the road. He grabbed his purchases and walked out of the store.

Kate scrolled through the photographs and video of her family on the camera. There were dozens of them. She scanned the control panel again and found a button with a trashcan icon. She pressed it over and over with her bill.

Deleting image flashed the message on the screen. This was going to take a few minutes. She didn't have a few minutes.

Through the open window of the truck, she heard the jingling of the convenience store door. Dirk was coming back.

CHAPTER FORTY-TWO

DIRK STRODE ACROSS THE PARKING LOT AND grabbed the door handle of his truck. He pulled it open and lifted his foot to step inside.

"Wait!" yelled a voice from the store. "Sir!"

Dirk left the door ajar and turned back to the store. The clerk waved a small piece of paper in the air.

"What?" asked Dirk, taking a step towards the clerk.

"I almost forgot. We have a promotion on bananas," said the clerk. "Buy a bunch, get a free scratch ticket."

Dirk shook his head. "I don't do scratch tickets," he said. "They rigged."

"But it's free."

"I don't want it," said Dirk. He turned to his truck.

"How can you not want it? Here, I'll scratch it for you."

"Scratch away." Dirk climbed into the cab and reached to pull the door closed.

"You won!"

"Really?" Dirk's eyes lit up. "What'd I win?"

"Twenty bucks!" The clerk held the ticket in the air. "Look!"

Dirk climbed out of his truck and grabbed the ticket.

"No kidding? I never win anything!"

"Congratulations," said the clerk.

Dirk slid the ticket into his shirt pocket. He'd redeem it after his interview and use it to buy himself a nice breakfast. He climbed back into his truck.

"Must be your lucky day, sir."

Dirk grinned and turned the key in the ignition. "Oh, I think you're right," he said as the engine roared to life. "'My lucky day.' Say, you got a TV in that store?"

"Yes, sir," said the clerk.

"Turn it on to *America This Morning* in about half an hour. See exactly what kind of lucky day I'm having."

Dirk pulled the door shut and put the truck in gear. As he pulled out of the driveway, he raised his hand to wave goodbye.

What a nutjob, thought the clerk, waving back.

He shook his head and walked back to the store. He hadn't even noticed the mallard waddling across the parking lot.

CHAPTER FORTY-THREE

KATE PUMPED HER WINGS HARD AND FAST, racing the sunrise back to camp. She was still in the air when the first ray of light broke over the horizon. Her feathered body began to tremble. Each flap of her wings made them more useless. She grasped at the air with what were becoming open fingertips. The ground rushed toward her as she tumbled from the sky.

"*Ooof!*" she cried, landing in a heap. She laid perfectly still on her back in the neatly trimmed grass behind a small country house.

All was quiet. Looking up, she saw streaks of sunlight stretching across the early morning sky.

Kate raised one arm, then the other. She turned her neck from side to side. For the second time in an hour, Kate decided she wasn't hurt.

She closed her eyes and smiled. What started as a chuckle grew into an uncontrollable belly laugh. She'd managed to erase all the pictures and video of her family from Dirt Bag's camera. They were safe.

She gasped as she remembered Wacka. Her injuries seemed pretty bad. Kate hoped her family had been able to help her.

"Who's out there?" called a voice from a dark window of the house. "Is there someone out there?"

It was only then that Kate realized she was naked. Her clothes were still crumpled in a heap in the clearing where she'd become a duck. She leapt to her feet and scurried into the woods.

It would be a long, cold walk home if she couldn't find any clothes. She trudged through the woods for nearly twenty minutes before finding a full laundry line. She dashed into the yard and pulled down the only two items that looked as if they would fit: an orange and yellow spotted skirt and a little boy's *Teenage Mutant Ninja Turtles* T-shirt.

A while later she discovered a pair of dirty old sneakers in someone's gardening shed. They were a few sizes too large, but by now her feet were so raw she was relieved to have any protection at all.

Kate decided to brave the road for the rest of her journey home. Though it would still be a long walk, she had nothing but time.

Her parents and family would be worried about her and whether she'd been able to find Dirt Bag. If the reporter *had* been able to tell the world about her family, they'd have no choice but to pack up and flee to a new spot, far away.

Kate shuddered at the thought. She'd never realized how much she loved this place until she thought she might have to leave it. But Kate had won. Dirt Bag was gone. She was elated.

CHAPTER FORTY-FOUR

"I DON'T EVEN KNOW WHERE TO START LOOKING for her."

Brian leaned forward in the passenger seat of the van, his eyes drifting back and forth scanning the trees as Lisa drove slowly down a dirt road.

"This is the direction Bobby said she flew," she said. "I really don't know how far she could have gotten. Or what trouble she could have gotten into with that reporter."

Brian didn't answer. His leg pounded up and down. His wife rested her hand on his knee to stop him from shaking.

"She's a big girl," said Lisa. "She'll be fine."

"I know," Brian replied. He didn't sound convinced.

They drove on. They took a few short detours down laneways and logging roads that veered off the main road. But they always returned, keeping on in the same direction Kate was last seen flying.

"I don't like this," said Lisa after another half hour of searching.

"Neither do I," said her husband, his eyes still scanning the trees.

Lisa slumped back into her seat, then quickly sat bolt upright. She'd spotted something further up the road. "There's someone walking ahead," she said. "Maybe they've seen something."

As they got closer, the figure walking down the road—despite the mismatched outfit—started to look familiar. Lisa pulled the van up alongside the young teenage girl with the cartoon T-shirt and bright skirt.

"Thank goodness we found you!" called Lisa out the driver's window. "Are you all right?"

"I'm fine," said Kate, running to the side of the van and sliding open the door. She climbed in and hugged them both. "Did Bobby and Grandma tell you about Marcus and the reporter?"

"Of course," said her father. "But we have to hurry back. Everyone is packing up camp. We've got to get out of here as soon as we can."

"We don't!" said Kate. "I did it. I erased the photos on his camera."

"How did you manage *that?*" asked her father.

Kate gushed out her tale as her mother drove toward home. As she finished, she leaned back in her seat and closed her eyes. She dreamed of the long nap she'd take when they got back to camp.

Her parents sat silently in the front seat.

"What's wrong? I did it! We can stay," said Kate. "*Ah-wooooo*, right? No packing. No moving."

Lisa pursed her lips. "That is really great, Kate. You've bought us some time. But we still have to go."

"What do you mean?"

"If this reporter knows where we live. He'll be back."

Kate deflated. Her mum steered the van into the driveway of camp.

"We've got to leave, Kate. I'm sorry," said Brian. "I know you liked it here."

"'Liked?'" repeated Kate. "You're talking like we've already left! Where will we go?"

"Well," began Lisa, "Bea is going to put us up for a while, at least until we find a place of our own. It'll be a tight squeeze, but she's got space for all of us." She paused a moment, then added, "And John."

"And John?" repeated Kate.

Well," said Brian, glancing from his wife to Kate, "John is going to come live with us."

Kate's jaw dropped.

"We can't just leave him here," said Lisa. "His father's gone."

"Are we sure he's not coming back?"

"It looks like it," said Brian.

Kate was breathing heavily. Leaving this place. Moving. Taking John with them. Her victory suddenly didn't seem so victorious.

"Hey, everything is going to be okay," said her dad. "It's been a few years since we've had to move, but don't worry." He smirked. "Your mum and I have done this before. We're actually kind of good at this."

Kate's mum parked the van next to a pile of suitcases and gear that had amassed in front of the cabin. Bea stood waiting for them.

"You're back!" said Bea, pulling Kate close as she stepped out of the van. "You are going to love it at my place. Katie, we are going to have so much fun. You'll see." Bea grabbed Kate's hands and pulled her towards her station wagon. "Hey, come here. I want to show you something."

They opened the front passengers' side door and peered inside.

"Look who gets to ride shotgun," said Bea.

There, resting in a nest made from an old blanket, was a bundle of brown feathers.

"Wacka!" said Kate. "You're okay!"

The duck raised her head.

"When Bobby found your parents and I in the woods, he was worried her wing was broken," said Bea. "But we had a good look at her, and I think she's okay. We managed to stop her bleeding about an hour ago. She's been resting ever since. That's one brave little duck."

"Oh, Wacka," said Kate, stroking the duck's feathers. "We'll take good care of you. You'll see."

Wacka laid her head back in her nest.

"How is our patient?" came a voice.

Kate and Bea turned to see Marge walking slowly from the cabin.

"Resting now, Mum, like you should be," said Bea.

"How are you, Grandma? Are you okay?" asked Kate.

"I'm fine," said Marge, rubbing her bandaged neck. She put an arm around Kate. "It'll take more than

Marcus to do me in." She turned to Bea and muttered under her breath. "I told you he was no good."

"Spare me, Mother," said Bea, retreating to the cabin. She passed Bobby and John on their way out, their arms full of bags.

"Hey, you made it!" said John. He dropped his load into the back of the van and greeted Kate. "What happened?" he said. "Did you find Dirt Bag?"

Kate repeated her story, a little less enthusiastically this time.

"So, what's going to happen with you?" Kate asked John.

He shrugged. "Dunno. Don't suppose Dad's terribly happy with me right about now." He looked thoughtful for a moment then perked up again. "But Bea says I can stay at her place with you guys. Cool, huh?"

Bea walked past as John spoke, carrying a load of laundry from the cabin. Kate couldn't help but notice John's gaze follow her as she stuffed towels into the back hatch of her car.

"Need a hand?" asked John eagerly.

Kate watched as he peeled away from their conversation to help Bea. So much had changed. So little had changed.

Kate stood by the cabin, feeling her world swirl around her. She looked at the familiar trees, lake, and sky that had been part of her home for nearly as long as she could remember. She watched as her family hastily tossed all their worldly possessions into the back of the van.

Kate would miss this place. But somehow, she knew she would be okay. She knew exactly who she was. Wherever she went, she would still be Kate.

Kate Wereduck.

"Are you going to help out here, Miss Duckie, or what?" called practical Marge as she headed back into the cabin for a fresh load of bedding and towels.

Kate wrapped her arms around her body to warm herself against the chill morning air.

"Coming, Grandma," she said. "Coming."

EPILOGUE

"WELCOME BACK TO *AMERICA THIS MORNING!*" said a man with silver hair and gleaming teeth. His phony smile beamed to millions of television sets around the world.

"I'm Waaaaayne Noostum. Coming up in this half hour, *Ah-wooooo!* It's a wolf of a story you don't want to miss."

A graphic of a wolf howling at the moon danced across the screen.

Noostum chuckled. "We're not talking about Hollywood-special-effects-and-makeup werewolves. We're talking about the *real* thing. Here on *America This Morning*, we have an exclusive look at the world's first evidence of werewolves. And, would you believe— a were*duck*? Joining me via satellite, from our studio in Canada, is Dirk Bragg. He's a reporter with *Really Real News*, and he's brought with him photographic evidence he says will knock your socks off. Good morning, Dirk."

"Good morning, Wayne," said Dirk. A box featuring Dirk's smiling face popped up on the screen beside the host.

"Now, I understand you barely got away from these werewolves with your life!"

"That's right, Wayne," answered Dirk. He slowly and dramatically told the story of his adventure.

Noostum gasped at all the right spots. He was riveted by the tale. Dirk couldn't believe how well this was going.

"That's quite a story," said Noostum as Dirk wrapped up, turning his gaze back to the camera. "And now, dear audience, for the proof. Dirk Bragg took digital photos and video of these amazing events last night, and I'm pleased to say, we can now share them with you. Our affiliate station in Canada just sent us the files, and—well—let's just take a look for ourselves. Dirk, shall we just roll the video?"

"Absolutely, Wayne," said Dirk with a grin. "Let it roll."

The picture on the screen jumped as the video began to play. The screen was mostly shadows. It was difficult to make out exactly what was going on.

An image came slowly into focus. A man was walking up the steps of what looked like the stage of a dimly lit bar. The audio track played the tinny opening notes of a country song.

"What's this?" said Noostum.

"Uh," said Dirk. "I'm not quite…sure. This might not be the right file."

"My producer says it's the only video in your camera, Dirk," said the host.

The figure on the stage walked into the spotlight. It was Dirk. He pulled a microphone into his hand.

"*My wheels belong to the roooad...but my heart belongs to yooooooooou!*" sang the Dirk in the video.

"No! This isn't it!" yelled Dirk.

"Oh, I get it. *Really Real News* strikes again." Noostum chuckled. "Right. A *wereduck*. You almost had me for a minute. Get this clown out of our studio."

"I swear!" yelled Dirk. "It was real! All of it! The werewolves! The duck! Everythi–"

The satellite feed went dark.

Noostum looked calmly at the camera.

"In other news," continued the host, "K9 justice! A dog took to the witness stand today in a bizarre trial that's rocking the legal world...."

ACKNOWLEDGEMENTS

Jacques Poitras, Margaret McPike, Karen Rawlines, and Marion Smith provided valuable feedback on the earliest drafts of *Wereduck*. Ben Carwana and Jessica Arbing were my test-kids: both had questions and suggestions that helped me shape the story as I was writing. Thanks to Penelope Jackson and Nimbus Publishing for seeing the potential in my manuscript, and to my editor, Whitney Moran, for turning it all into a book. Thanks also to the talented Jenn Embree, whose illustrations and cover art, when I first saw them, made me squee with glee.

Henry, Jane, and Alice are the three silliest kids in the entire world. We read together on the couch every night, and it's the best part of my day, every day.

Special thanks to Erin. If it weren't for her creativity, patience, support, and endless cups of tea, this book wouldn't have been possible.